Lori

SO-CFK-742

That Certain Girl

by Dorothea J. Snow

cover and decorations by Carol Wilde

A WHITMAN BOOK
Western Publishing Company, Inc., Racine, Wisconsin

WHITMAN is a registered trademark of
Western Publishing Company, Inc.

Copyright © MCMLXIV, by
WESTERN PUBLISHING COMPANY, INC.
Produced in the U.S.A.

Library of Congress Catalog Card Number 64-20791

Contents

1

A Worried Man!

"Oh, Eliza, little Liza Jane. . . ." The strains of the familiar song filled the Holston Recreation Hall and set the feet of the listeners tapping.

"You'll change," Jimmy Bryant murmured as he and the girl beside him rose from the front tier of spectators' seats. His voice was teasing, yet there was a serious ring in it, too. "You'll soon forget all about me and the old gang. Wait and see."

"Oh, no, I won't!" Teddy Taylor replied emphatically as they paused, awaiting the call. "I won't change and I won't forget."

Art Blake, the small, wiry man standing beside the record player on the platform across the hall, sang out, "Choose your nearest partner and square up."

Jimmy took Teddy's hand and, frowning slightly, led her out to the center of the floor. After some jostling they were joined by three other couples and formed a square. The others were friends and neighbors, Vivian Robinson and Lyle Manners, Carol Newby and Bill Ashby, and Ruby Hart and Terry Martin.

They made up the old gang Jimmy had mentioned, and their mood, like his, seemed subdued this evening. There was nothing of the lighthearted humor Teddy had always known.

What in the world was the matter with them, anyway? Teddy thought irritably. One would think they were watching a losing basketball game instead of dancing to lilting music.

Especially Jimmy! He bent over suddenly until his lips almost touched her ear and whispered fiercely, "I hope you don't change." His voice became almost wistful as he added, "I like you just as you are!"

A tremor of surprise raced through Teddy. The tone of Jimmy's voice put a lot of meaning into that remark. Why was he suddenly so intense?

Until now he had been just a boy who lived in the same neighborhood as she, one of a group of friends each of whom she liked equally well. Oh, she had dated him occasionally. Several times they had been a twosome at a movie, but mostly it had been with the gang.

There had never been any of that belonging to each other among the group, except for Viv and Lyle, who lately seemed to be spending most of their time together.

Was Jimmy leading up to something like that? Was he going to ask her to go out only with him? Was he going to tell her he wanted to date no one else? If so, she didn't know whether she should be glad or sorry. She liked Jimmy more than any boy she knew, and she didn't want to hurt him. But she did wish he would stop telling her that she was going to change.

Teddy had no intention of doing any such thing. She had told him so, several times. Couldn't he take her word for it?

> "Break into a line of four,
> Pin that line, four face four."

Viv faced Lyle, Ruby faced Terry, and Carol turned to Bill. Teddy's racing thoughts slowed her responses. She was a second late turning to stand before Jimmy.

At that moment she saw him for the first time as an extremely attractive boy. Scarcely two inches taller than she, he seemed more so because of his slender build and rod-straight posture. His skin, tanned to almost the exact shade of his slightly curling, chestnut hair, intensified the clear blue of his eyes. His lips, tight-pressed at the moment, could, on occasion, break into a smile that was absolutely infectious.

She wished he would smile now. In a feeble effort to make him do so, she looked up at him with eyes wide with a mixture of real and mock astonishment and cried, "Why, Jimmy Bryant! Do you want me to stay fifteen years old forever?"

"Pass through."

As they smoothly passed each other in the maneuver, his frown deepened and he muttered accusingly, "You know what I mean."

"Wheel and deal."

They reversed directions and he went on, "Pretty soon you'll be acting like you had never known us."

She batted her lashes deliberately. "Is that so? Seems to me you're pretty sure of a lot of things."

He didn't answer.

"Over and through, roll away
With half a sashay,
Box the gnat across the way."

As the others in the square whirled about her, Teddy sent plump, dark-haired Viv a warm smile. She laughed inside herself at Jimmy's prediction. She would forget Viv? Why, Viv had been her best friend ever since she could remember! Viv, in whose home next to her own on Colfax Street she had spent so many happy hours! With whom she had made mud pies, and played under sprinklers on hot days, and cut out paper dolls and their bright-colored clothes! With whom she had gone through kindergarten and grade school and junior high and was now sharing the fun and tribulations of high school!

Forget lovable, loyal Viv? Not in a million years! She would never forget any of her gang. Especially not Jimmy, though now he had swung around and was practically glowering at her.

He looked so funny. Impishly, she thrust her face close to his and stuck out her lower lip in what she hoped was comical determination.

"I will not forget *anybody!*" she hissed. "How can I when I will be here every Friday night same as always? You know I'd rather square dance than eat."

This was such an exaggeration that a smile flickered over Jimmy's face for an instant.

"Wheel and deal a quarter more."

Then, deadpan again, he went on, "So did your mama and papa once, but they don't come anymore."

Her brows arched. "Yours aren't here, either," she reminded him.

"They're visiting friends. That's the only reason they aren't here tonight."

"Well, my papa is just too busy."

It was the wrong reply, she knew that instantly. Jimmy shot back, "Oh, sure, I forgot. Your papa is a big-shot contractor now—building houses for all the new folks coming to Holston to work on the moon project."

"What's wrong with that?" she asked tartly, welcoming the next call.

"Pass through,
Outside four,
California whirl."

Gladly she whirled away from him. Happily she executed the next few steps with Bill Ashby. Bill was a tall boy with bristling hair. He said nothing, just grinned down at her in a sheepish sort of way. *He* didn't make her feel guilty. He had always treated her as someone special, too. She knew why and rather enjoyed it. The Taylor family was easily the most prosperous on Colfax Street. Their home had been remodeled and enlarged until it was now the biggest and most imposing house in the neighborhood; it was always freshly painted, with lawn mowed and hedges clipped. They alone employed a yardman full time. And every year at least one of their two cars was traded in on a new one.

For some time now Teddy had been the undisputed leader of the group on Colfax Street, and she liked the feeling. Everyone was always quick to agree to any suggestion she made. Only Jimmy sometimes put up an argument, disagreed with her, or questioned anything she did.

Tonight was a good example of that. He had no more reason to chide her than the others did. It had been common knowledge for several months that the Taylors were moving away from their old home on Colfax Street to a big new mansion on Holly Tree Hill.

Everyone had said they were sorry to see the Taylors move. But only Jimmy acted as though their moving was some kind of crime.

"Colfax Street will never be the same without the Taylors,"

some of the neighbors had remarked sadly, but that had been all. They had said nothing about the likelihood that the Taylors would go high-hat after moving into the swank world on the Hill.

The thought of the lovely new home Papa had built there brought a dreamy smile to Teddy's face. She remembered how, as a tiny girl, she had once thought that living on the Hill must be like having a home on the grounds of Windsor Castle in England or the Alhambra in Spain. Even now she was sure it was a place where folks lived in fantastic splendor with never a care or a problem.

Holly Tree Hill was an almost magical name in the Deep South city of Holston. A symbol of wealth and culture, it stood in the center of town with the rest of the city spread around it.

On the very top of the Hill stood the beautiful antebellum mansion known as the Martineaux house. It had been built over a hundred years ago by Andre Martineaux, a planter who had emigrated from Virginia, and his father who had become very wealthy by selling at high prices the huge tract of land he had acquired during the land sales of the early nineteenth century.

The house was now occupied by the widow of a direct descendant of those gentlemen, Mrs. Pierre Martineaux.

For many years Mrs. Martineaux had been the leader of Holston society. Now a white-haired, aristocratic-looking woman in her seventies, she was no longer active in social life, although she did still lend the prestige of her name to an occasional charity function.

She was sometimes called *Mrs. Moneybags,* but not without respect. She was a very wealthy woman, with real estate interests all over town. She attended to her affairs herself, being also a very good business woman. She could often be seen sitting austerely in the back of her long, black car while her chauffeur drove her from one meeting to another. Then, business over, she was driven back to the splendor of the big-columned house on the Hill.

Although some people envied her, others pitied the old woman. Many years before, her only son had left town and gone to live in California. He had never returned to Holston. Once each year, his mother would journey to visit him, and a few weeks later she would return, seemingly more lonely than ever.

That is, until her last visit. This time when she returned she brought her granddaughter with her. Now, everyone said, Mrs. Martineaux seemed to smile more often, though they would hasten to add that the granddaughter didn't seem very happy.

The dance ended and everyone slowly left the floor. Jimmy took Teddy's hand and led her back to the first row of seats.

"Coke?" he asked as she sat down.

"Ummm. Thanks. I am thirsty."

She wasn't really. But Jimmy had begun again to remind her how she would change after she had moved to the Hill. It would be good not to have to listen to that talk, even for the few seconds it would take him to go to the Coke machine and back.

Besides, she wanted to return to her thoughts of the coming move. The prospect was enough to thrill the most blasé, and she wasn't that, not even a tiny bit.

The Taylors *would* be moving up in the world. Their circumstances would certainly change. The modestly comfortable homes on Colfax Street were a far cry from the Martineaux house and the other elegant homes that lined the drive curving down and around Holly Tree Hill.

While visiting the house her papa was building for his

family on the last vacant lot there, Teddy had noticed that
there were two other antebellum homes in the neighborhood.
They were of the same era as the Martineaux house, but they
were smaller in size and were set in less spacious grounds.
She saw, too, several Victorian-styled mansions, marked by the
turrets and gables and other ornamental features of that period.
Mingled with these were homes of later periods, right down
to ranch types, split-levels, and colonials with modern touches.

An ice-cold bottle thrust into her hand interrupted Teddy's
thoughts. She took the bottle and began to sip.

She saw Art Blake motion to Jimmy and felt again a tiny
sense of relief for an interruption to the lecture she knew
Jimmy was going to continue.

She, as well as many others in the hall, knew what the motion
of Art's hand meant. She was not surprised to see two other
young fellows leave the crowd and make their way toward
the platform.

"Be seeing you," Jimmy said hastily as he set his half-empty
Coke bottle beside her on the seat and started for the platform,
too. She could tell by his eagerness to get there that his glumness
had vanished.

Her knowledge of what was coming brought a glow of
happiness to Teddy. And to Viv, also, who snuggled up beside
her and chortled, "Oh, boy! Jimmy and the boys are going to
sing! Honestly, they're getting better all the time. Don't you
think so, Ted?"

"Ummm." Teddy grinned at her and continued to sip her
drink. She tried to be nonchalant about this business of being
known as the girl friend of one so often called upon to sing
before groups like this. It set her apart, she knew, just like her
father's being one of the town's most prosperous contractors
set the family apart from the rest of the people on Colfax

Street. She liked the feeling, though she would never come out and say so.

"Ladies and gentlemen!" Art Blake's pleasant voice came over the microphone. "You're in for a real treat. The Jimmy Bryant Trio has consented to do a few numbers for us."

Teddy lowered her eyes and tried to think of nothing but the bottle in her hand. How mixed-up she felt at times like this! She thrilled with pride and yet she felt embarrassed, too. She loved to listen but she could not bring herself to lift her eyes and watch Jimmy perform!

She didn't know the other boys in the trio very well. They, like Jimmy, would be high school juniors in the fall, while she would enter as a sophomore. Only their names were familiar, since Jimmy had mentioned them often. They were Buddy Carr, who played banjo, and Glenn Curtis, who played bass.

Jim had organized the group and was its acknowledged leader. The boys played mostly for fun, but occasionally they were paid a small fee. Their repertoire consisted mainly of familiar folk and country numbers. Once in a while, however, they would work out one that was distinctly their own. Jimmy was good at writing new lyrics for old tunes and twisting old lyrics into numbers that sounded very new.

The boys picked up the instruments they had left beside the steps of the platform. Art stepped back and let them take their places before the mike.

Jimmy, guitar in hand, seemed very poised and confident as he introduced their first number.

"We'll start off with an old favorite, folks," he said. "It's called 'The Worried Man Blues.'" He grinned shyly and sort of shuffled his feet. "And when we get to the chorus we want everybody to join in. Just open your mouths and sing, and clap and holler, too, if you want to. Ready, boys?"

They played a few chords and then leaned forward. In surprisingly good voices they sang:

> "The train I ride is twenty-one coaches long,
> The train I ride is twenty-one coaches long,
> The train I ride is twenty-one coaches long,
> I'm worried now but I won't be worried long!"

Teddy raised her eyes. She could watch now that everybody was going to sing, including herself.

Singing and clapping and swaying gently to the rhythm of the old song, everybody joined in a real hootenanny.

> "It takes a worried man to sing a worried song,
> It takes a worried man to sing a worried song,
> It takes a worried man to sing a worried song,
> I'm worried now but I won't be worried long!"

The trio sang another verse and again everybody joined in the chorus.

They sang another verse and then another. Everybody was having a wonderful time, including Teddy. She did, that is, until they came to the last verse. Then she felt like a butterfly impaled on a board with a pin.

Jimmy's glance met hers just as the chorus ended and she looked down again at the Coke bottle in her hand.

He continued to look straight at her as they sang:

> "The girl I love is on that train and gone,
> The girl I love is on that train and gone,
> The girl I love is on that train and gone,
> I'm worried now but I won't be worried long!"

While the others sang and clapped through the last chorus, Teddy sat in a half daze. Jimmy had said he loved her, right out in front of everybody! She felt relieved when the last notes of the song died away and Jimmy turned his attention elsewhere.

But Viv wouldn't let the matter rest. She applauded vigorously, even after the others had stopped. Then she sighed noisily, "A worried man, that's Jimmy."

Teddy sent a surprised look her way and asked as coolly as she could, "For Pete's sake, why?"

Viv shrugged and made a mournful-looking face.

"His girl will soon be on that train and gone, he thinks," she said, adding softly, "and he's worried because he's afraid she'll forget all about him."

2

A Brand-New World

Teddy sat thoughtfully before the gold and white French provincial desk in her room in the new house on the Hill. Only seven days had passed since she and her family had moved; yet it seemed like a thousand years.

So much had happened—so much hustle and bustle and adjusting.

Tapping the white leather-bound blotter on top of the desk, she let her mind wander back over the events of their last day on Colfax Street. From the moment of her awakening that morning she had been eager to leave. But at the same time she had been filled with a sense of sadness, too.

She remembered the last loaded van pulling out of the driveway of their old home and Papa and Mama taking a final walk through the empty house.

She and Dixie, her ten-year-old sister, had followed them.

"It's the end of an era, I reckon," Papa had said as they started up the stairs. His voice had been charged with emotion, although he had tried to cover it with a jovial gruffness.

Teddy had thought then that with very little persuasion Papa would have called off the move and stayed in the house to which he had brought Mama as a bride.

It had been Mama who, outwardly calm and placid, had broken the tension. "And the beginning of another," she had said softly.

Papa had laughed then and taken Mama's hand. Leaning over, he had kissed her ear and said, "That's the best way of looking at it, I reckon."

Dixie had wiped away a big tear that was trickling down through her freckles, and Teddy had swallowed a big lump in her throat. She had been glad to hear Viv suddenly call from downstairs, "Anybody home?"

Teddy had run back down, leaving Mama and Papa and Dixie to continue their farewell tour.

She and Viv had been joined by Carol and Ruby. They had stood about for a few moments, self-consciously.

Viv had covered any sadness she might have felt with forced chatter. Carol and Ruby, as usual, had said little, though Teddy realized that behind their quietness the two girls were close to tears.

Neighbors had been dropping in all morning. Mrs. Robinson brought in a pot of coffee and a plate of doughnuts, and she had wanted to know if the family needed any last-minute help.

Jimmy had wandered over, too, from his father's grocery store on the corner of Colfax and Main. He was working there full time this summer as delivery boy.

Teddy had panicked when she saw him coming. Would he tell her, in front of her parents, that he loved her? While Mama and Papa thought he was a very nice boy, she knew they wouldn't approve of a serious relationship.

She had had no need to feel concerned, though. Jimmy had greeted her as he would have any good friend. And he had talked to the rest of the family as much as he had to her.

When it was time to leave Colfax Street, Jimmy had opened the car door and helped her in beside Dixie.

"Take care of yourself," he had grinned. "And watch your manners up there among the aristocrats."

Papa had chuckled at that. Jimmy had winked, pretending it was at Dixie, and slammed the door shut.

"So long," he had said to all of them. "Have fun."

Then he had stood in the driveway, with Viv who had just come out of her house next door, and waved as the big car had purred down the street.

By this time the lump that had been forming in Teddy's throat seemed to have grown to the size of a baseball. Dixie had seemed to be about ready to burst into tears, too, Teddy noticed. As the car had rounded the corner by the grocery store the silence in the front seat had become so obvious that baby Rick had looked up in round-eyed bewilderment from his perch on Mama's lap.

Even Elvira, their cook, had looked sad. Sitting in the back seat with Teddy, Dixie, and Dave, the oldest Taylor, she had looked down at the bird cage in her lap and shaken her head at the canary, Twinkie.

"It sho' will seem funny," she had said, "going up to that new house on the Hill to work."

In a few minutes, however, as the car began its slow climb up the Hill, the fog of gloom had begun to lift. Papa had grinned broadly as he had swung it into the wide, curving driveway leading to the handsome, new, twelve-room house.

It was an antebellum styled house with a portico across the front and round, fluted columns rising to the roof above. The sight of it, gleaming through the grove of huge trees on the grounds, had sent a thrill of pride through the entire family.

Busy days of getting settled had followed, with everyone

taking delight in the spaciousness of their new home. Each had a large room of his or her own. There was no crowding of belongings or furnishings.

"Boy, I can really spread out here," Dave had exclaimed as he had proceeded to stretch out on the couch in his own pine-paneled room overlooking the back garden. "This is really living."

He had sat up then, grinning in satisfaction at his surroundings. His was a large room furnished in a Western style that was masculine and meant for hard wear and comfort—just right for an athletic eighteen-year-old who would be a high school senior in the fall.

Dixie's room was all a ten-year-old lover of animals could want. The gay paper on its walls pictured scampering dogs, cats, squirrels, horses, and other four-legged creatures. The bases of two lamps were bronze dogs, and the hooked rug on the polished floor was centered with a stiffly stylized pony.

Yet Dixie was not completely happy about the move.

"Some home," she had sniffed several times during the first week. "No place for Cottonblossom."

"A home on the Hill," she had been reminded, "is no place for a *goat,* not even a special one like Cottonblossom."

But Dixie had continued to sneer at everything about the new home on the Hill.

Suddenly Teddy's thoughts came back to the present. Her face was a study of indecision as she continued to tap the blotter on her desk with the tip of her ball-point pen. Should she, or shouldn't she?

The problem had started the previous evening when Papa had remarked that it must be about time for her to ask some of her old friends to visit her in her new home.

So far no one from Colfax Street had come by or called. But

Teddy had been so busy that she hadn't given it much thought.

"I could have a party," she had said, thinking of the gay, informal affairs that had taken place in their recreation room on Colfax Street.

"Fine," Papa had agreed.

Dixie, as sometimes happened, had come up with a surprisingly good idea.

"How about a pool party?" she had asked, for a moment thinking of something besides her missing Cottonblossom.

Teddy's eyes sparkled.

"Say, why didn't I think of that?"

Dixie had wrinkled her pug nose and smirked. " 'Cause you're not as smart as I am, that's why," she had said matter-of-factly.

Papa, suppressing a grin, had assured Teddy, "The pool will be ready a week from Saturday. How about having the party then?"

"I'll just do that," she had replied.

She had plenty of time to get ready for it. First things first, she had told herself half an hour ago when she had sat down at her desk to address the invitations she had written last evening after dinner.

It was taking her much longer to address them than it should, and she knew it. But she simply could not make up her mind to do something she had wanted to do since the first night she had slept in her new room.

It would take courage, she told herself fiercely. It always took courage to be different.

Hastily she scribbled something on a piece of scratch paper, then scrutinized it closely. Yes, she decided, she would do it.

Blissfully she lifted her gaze and let it wander about her room. It was beautiful, she thought for the umpteenth time.

All the furnishings were new—French provincial in white and gold with touches of powder blue. Her bed was a dainty four-poster with canopy and spread of blue organdy. The polished floor was centered with a fluffy blue nylon rug that looked like spun sugar candy.

She had to pinch herself to realize the room was really hers, and not that of some fairy princess she had read about. She loved her new surroundings, though at first she had missed the old maple desk with its big drawers and scarred top that she had given to Viv.

Why hadn't Viv called her? Or Ruby? Or Carol? Why hadn't Jimmy tried to get in touch with her? They must realize that she had been too busy to call *them*.

Again she looked at the word she had scribbled on the scratch paper. *Teddi*. How much more in keeping it was with her new life than was the common *Teddy!*

Could she take the teasing that would surely follow such a change?

Still, it would only last a short time. And she would always have a name that was special, that set her apart.

Through her window, framed with sheer, ruffled white curtains, she saw the workmen putting some pipes into the big pool in the backyard. That did it! Anyone with a swimming pool in her backyard should have a name like Teddi!

Her shoulders straightened determinedly. She picked up the envelope on which she had written her return address, *Teddy Taylor, 2 Holly Tree Lane, Holly Tree Hill, Holston,* and tore it squarely in two. Then she tossed the pieces into the gold and white wastebasket that stood beside the desk.

She picked up another envelope. In the same spot on it she wrote *Teddi Taylor, 2 Holly Tree Lane, Holly Tree Hill, Holston.* Holding it at arm's length, she studied it happily.

Her real name was Thelma, but no one except Grandma Taylor ever called her that. For which she felt thankful now!

What a difference that small *i* made! It took the common nickname her father had given her when a baby and put it into the same class with, say, *Mimi,* which was the name of Mrs. Martineaux's granddaughter! Now that she lived in the same neighborhood as Mimi Martineaux, why shouldn't she be in the same class?

"You'll change!" Jimmy's words came back to her.

"I am not changing," she told herself fiercely. "I am only changing the spelling of my name."

That wasn't quite true, however. Ever since she had moved to Holly Tree Hill, she had had a strange, mixed-up feeling—like floating on a cloud while she tried to keep her feet on good, solid earth.

"Jumpin' jeepers! Haven't you finished those old invitations yet?" came a mocking voice from the doorway of her room.

Teddi sat bolt upright. Hastily she stuffed the envelope into a drawer of her desk. She slammed the drawer shut.

It just wouldn't do to let Dixie see that—not yet, anyway.

Teddi rose and turned. Her heart sank at the sight in the doorway. Dixie, an old air pump in hand, stood there looking like a cross between an orphan of the storm and a waif from the back country.

Teddi sighed inwardly. How she hoped that Mama and Dixie would soon realize that the women and girls on the Hill dressed differently than those on Colfax Street. Though none of their new neighbors had called on the Taylors yet, Teddi had done some observing from a distance.

She knew that everyday wear on the Hill was not faded, worn-out "good" clothes as it was on Colfax Street. Everyday clothes up here were called "casuals," and they were just as new and expensive as "dressy" things.

She eyed Dixie's frayed and faded jeans, her equally frayed and faded shirt, and mentally compared them with the crisp new pants and matching blouse of the small girl she had seen in the next yard.

"No, I haven't finished them," she replied, her eyes disapproving. Then she added, rather bitingly, "In the name of common sense why don't you neaten yourself up a bit?"

She bit her lip in vexation. *Neaten.* It was an old country expression she had heard Grandma Taylor use many times. But Grandma lived in the country where such expressions were common. Here on the Hill such talk as that would flash her newcomer status like a neon sign. And she didn't want that.

Dixie gave a mild hoot.

"Ya'll mean like this?" she snickered and slipped her fingers through her already-stringy hair, back to front, producing a sort of Medusa-like effect. Then, letting the pump slip to the floor, she stuck both hands into the pockets of her frayed jeans. Lifting the cuffs halfway up her skinny legs, she minced about the room.

Teddi laughed in spite of herself. Dixie was a clown— lovable, though sometimes exasperating. Then she quickly wiped the smile off her face. It didn't do to encourage Dix. That was made plain when the little imp queried, "Why don't you call the kids on the phone and ask them to your party? That's the way you used to do it."

Teddi turned back to her desk, snapping, "Oh, get lost, will you?"

Dixie did, but only after she had pranced around the room between Teddi's desk and her window, crowing, "Boy, are we getting hoity-toity! And touchy!"

Teddi leaned threateningly across the desk and tried to grab her sister. Whereupon Dixie dodged her outstretched arm and streaked out of the room, picking up the pump as she went.

Teddi plumped back down in her chair. So Dixie thought she was changing, too. Well, maybe she was a bit—outwardly. Deep down inside, she assured herself, she was the same Teddy Taylor she had been on Colfax Street.

She was inviting the same kids to her pool party that she would have invited to a party on Colfax Street, wasn't she?

From her desk drawer she retrieved the envelope she had thrust there. In the lower right-hand corner she wrote Miss Vivian Robinson, 506 Colfax Street, Holston.

She quickly addressed fifteen more, signed and slipped an invitation into each one, and sealed them.

3

With All Her Heart

Teddi stamped the envelopes.

"I'll take them down to the mailbox right away," she decided. "The kids must get them early so they will have plenty of time to make plans to come."

Everyone she was inviting would come, Teddi was sure of that. No one would turn down a party on the Hill—and a pool party at that. This was probably the first pool party any of them had ever been invited to. She knew none of them had pools in *their* backyards. They were lucky to know someone who did.

Another thought gave her pleasure. They would be so pleased to receive their invitations that they would probably not even notice she had changed the spelling of her name. It would be better if the realization dawned upon them gradually.

With increasing delight her gaze took in the oval-shaped pool in the backyard. It was set on the first of several terraces that stepped down back of their house until stopped by the retaining wall of the ranch-type house lower on the slope. Beside the pool was a colorful cabana around which a man was now setting out shrubs.

Papa had called the pool a teen trap. It was easy to see he hoped it would be. He and Mama had always made a great effort to provide recreation facilities at home for their children and their friends. The big recreation room in the basement of their old home on Colfax Street had been the only one of its kind in the neighborhood. It had always been filled with laughing, noisy boys and girls.

"The pool should make it easier to become acquainted with the young folks here on the Hill," he had said several times. "All you will have to do is ask them over for a dip. After that they'll likely be swarming over here."

Teddi hadn't been so sure about that. But she hadn't said so. Papa simply didn't know that things were different on the Hill.

The recreation room had been a novelty on Colfax Street. But every house here on the Hill probably had a swimming pool. It would take more than such a commonplace thing to open the doors of friendship on Holly Tree Hill.

Nancy Moore could certainly see the pool being built, and *she* hadn't given Teddi so much as a friendly wave.

Nancy was the brightly blond girl who lived in the big Tudor-style mansion next door that looked so impressive from the street. Twice during the past week Teddi had seen Nancy. She had hoped the blond girl would give some sign of friendliness, but she hadn't given any indication of even noticing her new neighbors.

Teddi hesitated to wave first. Nancy's father was a well-known lawyer in town and a prominent figure in the county courthouse. And every few days, it seemed, Mrs. Moore's picture appeared on the society page of the *Holston Times*. Nancy herself attended Holston Academy, a private school out on Old Coach Road. One didn't treat such people as these in the casual way one treated the neighbors on Colfax Street!

Teddi especially remembered Nancy as a hostess at one of the handsome, antebellum homes opened to the public during the city's annual Blossom Time Festival. She and Viv had bought tickets for the Pilgrimage, as the tour through the old houses was called. Along with many others they had gazed with awe at the houses *and* the young ladies who stood about lending color, answering questions, and acting as guides. In the hoopskirts and floppy hats of the period before the War Between the States, they had looked like colorful butterflies flitting about the beautiful homes.

"It must be a lot of fun to be one of those hostesses," Teddi had remarked as she and Viv had watched Nancy gracefully posing for a picture beside a flowering crape-myrtle bush.

Viv had popped her gum rather noisily and replied, "I s'pose it is." Then she had shrugged and added, "But we live in the wrong part of town to be picked for something like *that*."

"You're so right," Teddi had sighed a bit wistfully.

She and Viv had exclaimed over the lovely formal gardens and majestic interiors of the Shuttleworth house. They had wandered down paths white with crushed shells and edged with neatly clipped hedges of boxwood and holly. Then they had toured the twenty-four rooms, exclusive of the servants' quarters, and had sunk ankle-deep, it seemed to them, in the rugs that covered the polished, wide-board floors.

Now, Teddi thought, she did live in the right part of town to be chosen a hostess for this summer's festival. The very thought made her heart beat quicker. Then it slowed. Hers was probably the same sort of wishful thinking that Papa had been doing about the pool as a teen trap. One had to become acquainted with those in charge of such things before one was even considered.

Having a friend like Nancy would be a good beginning.

But would she and Nancy ever become good friends? Desperately she hoped that they would soon become as close as she and Viv had always been.

Oh, no, she shouldn't think like that! No one could *ever* be as close a friend as Viv. Or could one have two close friends, without one taking the place of the other?

Well, she thought unhappily, so far she had no reason to be concerned about such a possibility. Riffling through the envelopes, she made certain the addresses were correct. So far she wasn't on speaking terms with Nancy—or anyone else on the Hill!

As a matter of fact, she was beginning to wonder if she had any close friends at all. Viv hadn't called her since the move; no message had come from her since the day she had stood in the yard of the old house and waved good-bye.

Shaking such thoughts from her head, Teddi went to her closet and picked out a skirt and blouse with the right kind of casually expensive look she felt was needed for the walk to the mailbox. There was no way of knowing whom she might meet going down the Hill and back. Sometimes a chance encounter could lead to wonderful things. And she wanted to be ready for any eventuality.

It just might serve Viv right if she happened to lose her invitation on the way! Still, she wanted the party to be a success, and Viv was a big help in that department. Always noisy and full of fun, Viv could liven up the dullest group.

Teddi smoothed the deep pleats in her beige skirt and inspected the round collar of the coordinated print blouse. Both were of slubbed silk and well tailored—just right, she thought with real satisfaction.

Invitations in hand, she swept down the stairs and out across the portico. Was she on the threshold of an exciting experience?

It was a nice thought. She turned it over and over in her mind while walking slowly down the concrete walk from her house. Its pleasure deepened as she stepped along on the old, red-brick sidewalk that edged both sides of Holly Tree Lane. Worn by the feet of residents for over a hundred years, the walk was now a prized antique that present residents said they would never replace.

It was a matter of deep pride with them.

Teddi felt the same pride seeping into her. It was a wonderful thing to live in such a neighborhood, with its pleasant blending of a leisurely, romantic past and a brightly modern present. Somehow at the moment it seemed she had always lived here. Colfax Street was distant, both in time and space, as though pushed back by an invisible hand.

Suddenly Teddi returned to reality with a bang. If she had always lived here, she would have friends in the houses along the street ahead. And she had none. Suddenly she felt very lonely. She hoped desperately she would meet some of her new, young neighbors today.

She passed the Moore home where two small children played on the lawn with a big, butter-colored collie.

Their names were Tom and Tina. Dixie had learned this the day after the Taylors' move to the Hill. They were Nancy's small brother and sister. They were twins, Dixie had added, and a couple of corkers.

"How did you find out so much so fast?" Teddi had asked of her own small sister, wondering at the same time what the Moores had thought of Dixie, dressed in her usual ragtag manner.

"Their ball came over into our yard," Dixie had explained, "and I threw it back. Then I followed it and played some ball with them. Hot diggity! That's a swell dog they have. I told 'em that I was going to dognap it."

She had giggled noisily at her own wit.

Teddi had shuddered. Dixie had no idea of the proper way to make friends up here. Her blundering tactics wouldn't succeed any better than Papa's teen trap.

No wonder the twins ignored her as she walked by their house today. They had probably been warned to stay away from such rough characters as the newcomers next door! How glad she was that Dixie wasn't with her now to spoil any opportunity she might have to make a good impression.

She passed a brick, ranch-type house. It was newer than the Moore house but not as new as her own. A family named Harris lived there, she remembered. A boy on a power mower was the only person visible in that yard, and he was probably a yard boy. She was certain no Harris would perform so menial a task.

Through an arbor covered with red rambler roses she caught a glimpse of a floppy hat and a pair of white gloves. That was probably Mrs. Harris gathering flowers to arrange in the house, probably the hardest work any Harris would be likely to be seen doing.

The lady was too far away and too busy to notice Teddi going by.

Across the street a car door slammed and a sleek car backed out of the driveway. The dark-haired, patrician-looking lady who was driving must be the mother of Tess Graves, Teddi thought. It would be nice having Tess for a friend. Tess was a junior at Holston High, same as Jimmy. He had occasionally mentioned her name with others he had jokingly called the "spoiled rich." Certainly she was in the top social crowd, and Teddi remembered that she had been a hostess at the Holk-Higgins house during the last festival.

Tess's mother was so intent on her driving that she didn't even notice Teddi.

Some progress she was making, Teddi thought dismally as she dropped the invitations into the mailbox. She had reached it without having been noticed by *anybody*. During a similar trip on Colfax Street, she thought a bit wistfully, she would have been hailed half a dozen times and stopped to talk to at least half that many.

Suddenly a figure coming around a flowering shrub that hung halfway across the walk startled her. Then her heart began to pound. What luck! It was Mimi Martineaux. There wasn't anyone on the Hill she would rather have for a friend.

For over a month she had toyed with that possibility. In fact, she had dreamed of it since the day Mimi had, surprisingly enough, registered at Holston High. Knowing she would soon be Mimi's neighbor had lent even more excitement to the Taylors' move to the new house on the Hill.

Tongues had wagged at Holston High when Mimi had first appeared at school.

"Why did she come to live with her grandmother?"

"Were her parents killed in a plane crash or something?"

"Or divorced?"

Their curious questions were never answered. The tall, quiet girl had kept strictly to herself. Soon the talk had died down and they left her alone.

But Teddi never gave up hope of becoming her friend.

Mimi and Teddi! Like it had been *Teddi and Viv!* To be so linked with the granddaughter of Mrs. Pierre Martineaux was a possibility that took her breath away!

This didn't mean she was changing her attitude toward Viv, either. It was just that Mimi lived close by while Viv was now far away. After all, one did have to adjust to new surroundings.

Mimi was obviously returning from one of her frequent trips to the library, for she was practically staggering under the weight of the books she carried.

Twice during the past week Teddi had seen Mimi pass the house, and each time she had been so loaded down. Twice Teddi had hurried out, hoping the tall girl would see her and speak. But both times Mimi had been out of sight by the time she had reached the front yard.

Breathlessly now she stood and waited. Mimi *had* to see her this time, for she was coming straight toward her and the mailbox.

Should she wait for her, then speak casually, and fall into step beside her for the walk up the Hill?

Already she could hear Mimi saying in that deep, throaty voice of hers, "Can you spare a few minutes? Come on up to my house."

Trying not to appear too eager, Teddi would reply, "Why, yes, I think I can come. Wait until I run in and tell Mama where I'm going."

She would run into her house and . . . well, that would be the correct way to make a friend here on the Hill.

Should she wait for Mimi? No. That would make her plans too obvious.

I'll walk slowly back toward home, she told herself. *She will catch up with me. She can't walk past without saying something.*

Mimi was only half a block away now and on the same side of the street. Sun glinting on her auburn hair, she walked, head down, with no apparent interest in anything about her. If she heard the redbird scolding from the top of a fat cedar tree, she gave no sign. Nor did she seem to notice the mass of fragrant climbing roses covering an ancient stone wall she passed, or see the gray squirrel that skittered across the walk in front of her.

She must remember me, from school and all, Teddi thought as she turned to make her way, at a snail's pace up the Hill. *She'll probably be surprised to find I live so close by.*

All the way up, past the Harris and the Moore homes, her ears were tuned to the sound of footsteps coming nearer and nearer behind her.

But the sound did not come. She reached the walk that led to her own home and Mimi had not overtaken her.

Turning in toward her own house, she flicked a glance back down the red brick sidewalk. Mimi was there, all right— walking, head down, the same distance behind her that she had been at the mailbox.

The realization of what had happened stung Teddi. Mimi had known who she was, and where she lived. She had purposely walked just as slowly as Teddi, so as *not* to catch up with her.

Teddi ran into the house. She agreed with Dixie now. She didn't like this old Hill, either. With all her heart she wished she were living back on Colfax Street where people weren't so hoity-toity.

4

Tender Thoughts

Teddi could have screamed with joy at the sound of Jimmy's voice from the kitchen. But she didn't.

She decided not to let him know how fiercely she missed him and the old gang. In spite of everything, she had too much pride for that. So she checked her headlong rush toward the rear of the house after Mimi's brush-off and struggled to get control of her emotions.

While she slowed her pace to a saunter she heard Elvira's chuckle. "Go 'long with you, boy. That's the same ol' cake you bin eatin' in ma kitchen since you was knee-high to a grasshopper!"

Jimmy's bantering reply delighted Teddi. "Now, Elvira, you can't fool me. I know this is some superduper cake you've learned to bake since the Taylors moved up here on the Hill. Ummm. It's the best cake I ever put in my mouth."

Teddi stopped just before she reached the doorway to the kitchen and suppressed a giggle. Jimmy was up to his old tricks. When eating, no matter what kind of food, he always said it was the best he ever put into his mouth. Such flattery had made him the favorite of all the women on Colfax Street, and Elvira had been no exception.

Taking a deep breath, Teddi walked sedately into the room. Elvira was unpacking the contents of a big carton of groceries onto the kitchen table. Jimmy was sitting on a stool at the counter eating a big wedge of thickly frosted cake.

"Well, hi, Jimmy," Teddi said as casually as she could, considering the fact that she really felt like hugging and kissing him. "Long time, no see."

Jimmy turned slowly on the stool and eyed her warily.

"Yeah, it has been a long time, hasn't it?" Then he went back to his cake, cutting off a generous piece with his fork.

Teddi walked toward the rest of the banana cream cake Elvira had baked. She cut herself a piece and lifted it onto a small plate. Then from a drawer she took a salad fork, carried both to the stool beside Jimmy, and sat down. All the while she knew that Jimmy was groping for something else to say to her, just as she was trying to think of another light remark to make to him.

The whole thing seemed odd. Small talk had come so easily to them when she had lived on Colfax Street.

Teddi cut a tiny piece of the cake with her fork and ate it slowly, not even tasting it. Casually she remarked, "I've been wondering why you hadn't stopped by."

Jimmy took another bite of cake, his face a picture of deep thought.

"I was waiting for somebody to ask me," he said avoiding her eyes. He looked out the window toward the Moore house, then he gulped. "So, when Elvira phoned the grocery order this morning and said she wanted *me* to deliver it personally, I came."

Teddi swallowed another piece of cake. So that was why, during the past week, Joe Hardin, a clerk in the store, had delivered their groceries—not Jimmy. Well, she wasn't going to tell him how disappointed she had been in not seeing him behind the wheel of the truck.

At that instant something on the stove demanded Elvira's attention. So that was it! Elvira had sensed her feelings and done something about it. But would Elvira admit it? Oh, no!

"I jest don't like the way that Joe sets the box down on the table—smash, like that!" the woman said, stirring the contents of a pan with great vigor.

"Oh, you don't need to make excuses, Elvira," Jimmy said, with a quick glance in her direction. "I was glad to come."

Jimmy didn't grope for words when he talked to the cook, Teddi noticed. What had happened between them? What had caused this strained feeling? Why couldn't she tell him she had missed him? Forgotten was the scolding he had given her at the dance. All she could remember were the good times they had had. But she couldn't bring herself to say the desired words.

"I didn't think anybody had to ask you to come to our house," she managed to murmur.

Jimmy gulped down the last bite of cake, then picked up the empty carton from the table. He paused a moment before leaving. "I didn't think anybody ever visited anybody up here unless he'd been sent an engraved invitation," he said clearly. "And that brought to him by the butler!"

He was gone before Teddi could think of a reply to that.

She sat for a few minutes, forlornly, the rest of her cake uneaten. She missed the fellowship of the kids from the old neighborhood, Jimmy included. Would she ever experience anything like it among the young folks on the Hill?

A wave of longing for the old days, and the old friends, swept over her. Why didn't any of them call or come by?

Suddenly she sat up straight. Probably their reasons were the same as Jimmy's; they hadn't been asked!

Well, thank goodness, she had just remedied that situation. Tomorrow each of them would receive not an engraved invitation delivered by the butler, but a handwritten one delivered by the mailman. She picked up her fork and finished the cake, which suddenly seemed delicious. Tomorrow her friends would begin calling and dropping by to discuss the coming pool party. Those she didn't know well enough for that—some were acquaintances from school and church—would probably write polite notes of acceptance.

The rest of the day Teddi's thoughts were pleasant ones. As she helped Elvira set the table, played with Ricky, and listened to her favorite records before going to bed, she thought often of the coming calls and visits and notes—and Jimmy. Hardly once did she think of Nancy Moore or Mimi Martineaux or any of their other neighbors on the Hill.

She practically sat by the telephone all the next day, in a position where she could watch the front door, too. But not one single call did she receive, and not one visitor did she see!

Still, it was early, she reminded herself. *Tomorrow* she would receive all sorts of calls and visits *and* acceptance notes.

But the next day passed without any calls or visits from her old friends. And there were no notes of acceptance in the mail. She ate her dinner listlessly that evening, and then spent the rest of the night alone in her room.

The next day the same thing happened. Teddi suddenly felt a touch of panic. Wasn't *anybody* coming to her party?

"Why don'tcha call 'em and ask if they know what R.S.V.P. means?" Dixie asked without warning that evening. In her usual uncanny way her sister had sensed what was wrong with her.

"Perhaps I should." Eagerly Teddi grasped at the possibility. Then she thought of Viv.

"I may be stupid but I'm not dumb," was one of Viv's favorite expressions. If she called, Viv would be sure to say something like that. So Teddi gave up that idea.

"Oh, they know what it means," she said to Dixie with a hopeless gesture.

But in spite of everything she didn't give up hope. When she returned from a short visit to Grandma Martin's two days later, Elvira told her that Jimmy had stopped to deliver groceries again and had mentioned the party. So she knew the postal department hadn't mislaid the invitations.

"Did he say he was coming?" she asked quickly.

"No, and I didn't ask," Elvira replied. "I jest took it for granted he was."

So Teddi took it for granted the others were coming, too. But the next day the feeling of panic returned. Should she call them and *ask* if they were coming? No, she decided firmly. She wouldn't beg them to come—not even Jimmy!

Three days before the date set for the party Teddi sat at lunch with the rest of the family. She could hardly eat the food in front of her. The mailman sometimes came by during their lunch hour, and she wanted to be the first to reach the mail drop in the front hall. So far this week she had been first to riffle through the letters and see if there were any addressed to Miss *Teddi* Taylor.

Besides all her other anxieties, she was anxious that none of her family see the new spelling of her name, at least not yet! She felt badly enough without any of the teasing which would surely follow that.

She had wished a thousand times that she had not changed that *y* to *i*. She was convinced it had made her friends think she had become high-hat. And that was the reason she hadn't heard from any of them, she was sure.

But Jimmy had seen her and talked to her since she had moved. He should know she hadn't changed, not even a tiny bit. Yet, except for the grocery delivery instigated by Elvira, she hadn't heard from him, either. Everything was so confusing.

She strained her ears for the sound of footsteps on the portico and the slipping of mail through the brass-lidded chute. Did Papa have to talk so loud?

"I drove right past the house this morning," Mr. Taylor boomed in the hearty voice so characteristic of him. "I simply can't seem to realize that the Tate Taylors live in this fine big house on the Hill."

"Nor can I," Mama agreed, her soft brown eyes sweeping around the lovely dining room. "It is so much more than I ever expected to have."

Teddi wished that her parents wouldn't be so obvious about not being accustomed to all this luxury. What would Mimi and Nancy think if they heard such talk? What was happening to her? she asked herself sternly. Had she forgotten Mimi's unforgivable deed? But if her old friends were going to fail her. . . . She thought again of how she had hoped they would come to her party. What fun it would have been to show them her beautiful new home and pool.

Tap, tap. Was that the mailman crossing the portico? Did Dixie *have* to pick that second to scream, "Well, I liked it better on Colfax Street!"?

No, it wasn't the mailman. Teddi relaxed a little.

"Only because you could keep Cottonblossom there," Dave suggested with a big-brother grin.

Dixie scowled at him and then turned to her father. "You

could've built a shed for her in those old crape-myrtle bushes by the pool," she grieved. "Nobody would've known she was around."

"Until she baaed," Papa reminded her gently.

Teddi picked at a lettuce leaf. How could anyone miss a goat? No one but Dixie, she concluded. Dixie could form the greatest attachment for any kind of animal. Any stray creature that happened by the Taylor house was sure of a hearty meal and temporary shelter if Dixie was about. And she was always scouring the neighborhood for homes for her orphans.

"Baaaa!" Ricky crowed, thumping the tray of his high chair gleefully. Everybody laughed at that, including Teddi.

"Dixie takes after my mama," Papa had often said. "Ever since I was a little shaver I can remember Mama having an animal or two in the kitchen, feeding them with eye droppers, or bandaging legs, or something like that."

Dixie vowed she was going to be a veterinarian when she grew up. Neither Papa nor Mama tried to talk her out of that. But they had both given a firm "No" to her plea to bring Cottonblossom to the Hill.

"Colfax Street was on the outskirts of town," they argued, "and it was all right to keep a goat there. But Holly Tree Hill is in the center of town. It is no place for her."

So Papa had loaded Cottonblossom into one of his trucks and taken her to his parents' farm.

Now Papa patted Dixie on the head. "Living in this fine home should help you get over missing Cottonblossom," he said softly. While Dixie gave a soft sniffle he turned to the others and said proudly, "I always wanted my family to have the best."

Each member of the family knew how hard Papa had worked to achieve that ambition. When the moon boom had started in Holston, he had been a carpenter. As Holston had prospered, so had he, moving up to foreman of a construction crew, and then to contractor and head of his own construction company.

Construction was big business in Holston now. New workers, including hundreds of engineers and scientists, were pouring into the town every day. And they all demanded places to live. Motels were springing up like mushrooms, and subdivisions were appearing in what had been cotton and corn fields not too long ago.

Holston was the site of huge, sprawling Redwing Arsenal, and many other establishments related to the space effort. What had once been a big cotton mill now housed branches of several aircraft industries. The busy parkway that skirted one side of town was lined with offices of the space flight center, engineering companies, and research personnel. Cars and trucks with N.A.S.A. and U.S. Army lettered on their sides buzzed about everywhere. Famous government and military figures from all over the world were frequent visitors. Only two days ago someone had reported seeing two of the most recent astronauts in a store downtown, and the President himself had even made several stops. Holston was indeed playing an important part in creating the ships that would someday put an American on the moon.

The town was busy and bustling, and the Taylor Construction Company was going right along with it.

Was that the put-put of the mailman's little scooter? Teddi thought anxiously. No, it was just a noisy car going uphill.

The mailman didn't always come during the noon hour, she reminded herself. Sometimes he came afterward. But one couldn't be sure. So Teddi remained alert all during the rest of the meal.

She was glad when Papa and Dave went off in one of Papa's trucks. She sighed with relief when Mama and Dixie and Ricky disappeared down the driveway to visit Grandma Martin. Now she could wait for the mail in peace.

She wandered out onto the portico. Sitting down in a white wrought-iron chair, she gazed out over the tops of the bright red geraniums blooming in the long white planters set along the edge of the portico.

Would Mimi pass again this afternoon on her way to the library? Should she wave at her if she did? She decided to try again to become friendly with the Martineaux girl. During the past few days she had made all sorts of excuses for the girl's strange ways.

After a few moments of watching she decided that Mimi wasn't coming by that afternoon. So she rose and wandered into the house. Wouldn't the mailman ever come?

"What's for supper, Elvira?" she asked as she went into the kitchen."

"Black-eyed peas," Elvira replied as she put the last lunch dish into the dishwasher, turned the dial, and set it roaring. "And all the rest of yo' Papa's favorite vittles—ham, salad, and corn bread. Why?"

"I thought I might help with something."

"An' you sho' can. You can shell peas."

So Teddi sat down at the kitchen table, a big pan of unshelled peas on one side and a saucepan on the other. While Elvira bustled about and the peas rattled into the pan, she waited.

Ten minutes later she jumped up suddenly as Dave's roar came from the vestibule. "Is there a Miss Ted-eye Taylor in the house?"

"Oh, no," Teddi moaned. The worst had happened!

A glance out the window revealed a truck with TAYLOR CON-

STRUCTION COMPANY lettered boldly on its cab door. Dave had returned for some tool or other and she had not heard the motor of the truck because of the dishwasher's roar. He had seen the mailman coming and had beaten her to the mail!

Elvira's shoulders shook as she chuckled, "Ted-eye? Now what's that boy talking about anyhow?"

If you don't know you'll never hear it from me, Teddi thought grimly as she threw a handful of unshelled peas into the big pan and started toward the front door.

"Well, hello, Miss Ted-eye!" Dave cried at sight of her, his blue eyes crinkling at the corners just like his father's did. He handed her a single envelope.

"Well, hello yourself!" Teddi hissed, thinking it was just like Dave to pronounce *Teddi* like that. Grabbing the letter, she fled for the enclosed patio at the rear of the house.

She smarted from her brother's teasing, but a fast glance at the writing on the envelope made her feel better. She'd know Jimmy's scrawl anywhere.

Good old Jimmy, she thought tenderly. She should have known she could count on him.

Sitting down in a chair, she drew the envelope from her apron pocket where she had thrust it on her flight down the hall. Tenderly she smoothed out the wrinkles. Then she looked at it more closely. Suddenly she stiffened.

There on the envelope, as large as possible without running off the edge, Jimmy had written, *Miss Ted-eye Taylor, 2 Holl-eye Tree Lane, Holl-eye Tree Hill, Holston.*

In the upper left hand corner he had written, *Jimm-eye Br-eye-ant, 628 Colfax Street, Holston.*

Teddi sat a moment, seething with anger. Jimmy would do this to her! It was his crude way, she supposed, of bringing her down to size. Well, she'd waste no more thoughts on *him.*

5

Country Folks

The next day was Elvira's day off. It was also the day that Grandma and Grandpa Taylor made their weekly shopping trip to Holston.

They came in from their farm home near Redwing Crossing, a small mountain community about thirty miles from Holston. As usual they stopped first at their son's home to leave fresh vegetables and eggs—and chat.

They had stopped just as Papa was leaving for work. As always when that happened, Papa postponed his departure and insisted his parents sit down for a bite. Mama joined them and soon the four of them, with Ricky sitting in Mama's lap, were enjoying cake and coffee.

Teddi, her ears tuned to their conversation and her mind on Jimmy's note, was forlornly putting the breakfast dishes into the dishwasher.

That smart aleck Jimmy Bryant! She slammed a plate into the machine with such force that Mama looked her way in surprise. How could she be anything but angry with every word of that note etched in her memory where she could mentally read it over and over?

Dear Tedd-eye, it said. *Eye will be at your part-eye at seven sharp Saturda-eye. But wh-eye the note? Phone out of order? This repl-eye is costing me five cents and that is a lot of mon-eye to a poor bo-eye like me. Your old budd-eye, Jimm-eye.*

Some reply it was to her nice invitation! But it was the only one she had received.

Wasn't anyone coming to her party besides him? How discouraging! And the conversation from the table did nothing to brighten her frame of mind.

"It could make us rich," Papa was saying, "or it could land us in the poorhouse."

"Po'house!" Ricky crowed, clapping his fat hands in delight. Mama kissed his ear and cut herself another piece of Elvira's rich, hickory-nut coffee cake. Teddi sighed silently. No wonder Mama was becoming so plump.

That thought darkened her gloomy mood even more. She'd never have a mother like the slim, chic Mrs. Moore she had seen yesterday!

Unaware of her daughter's disapproval, Mrs. Taylor spoke up. "I wouldn't mind not getting rich, but I certainly don't want to lose everything we have, either."

Now what did Mama mean by that? Were they going to lose this lovely home before they had had a chance to really enjoy it?

Papa spoke up hastily. "Now I don't want to panic anybody." Then he shook his head and added, "I just reckon when a body plays with fire, he sort of figures he might get burned."

Teddi closed the door of the dishwasher with a little bang. Papa and Grandma and their platitudes. It seemed they had one to fit every occasion. Teddi sighed inwardly. She had visited the Moore house yesterday afternoon, and she hadn't heard such talk there.

Oh, she hadn't been invited, and she hadn't seen or talked to Nancy. She had simply gone to tell Dixie, who was playing with the twins, that it was suppertime and that Elvira had said she wouldn't wait forever to serve the evening meal.

Mrs. Moore had nodded at her. She was a woman in her late thirties who fairly oozed youthfulness. Not at all like Mama—who was so placid, and, well, colorless.

With two other chic ladies Mrs. Moore had been sitting on the patio at the rear of her home. They had been sipping tall, cool fruit drinks and discussing the latest fashions and hairdos.

Teddi wished Mama and Papa were like that—college-educated and smooth, with something else to talk about besides losing everything and going to the poorhouse.

There weren't such things as poorhouses these days, anyway. Though there had been when Grandma was young, she supposed. Papa had picked up the expression from his mother, as he had so much of his speech.

"Houses ain't selling in Mountainside Estates like you thought they would, eh, boy?" Grandpa's voice was thin and shrill.

"No, sir, they're not," Papa replied frankly.

Teddi wished he'd stop saying "sir" and "ma'am" to everybody. It sounded so countryish.

Papa went on, "I've built two split-level houses there—air-conditioned, with fireplaces and everything these new folks coming into Holston seem to demand. Got a lot of money tied up in 'em, too, believe me. But they just won't move."

Teddi flicked on the dial of the dishwasher, then turned to watch Papa carefully measure three teaspoonfuls of sugar into his fourth cup of coffee, and stir it vigorously. She waited while he took a tentative sip and said with a shake of his graying head, "I can't figure out why they don't sell. I picked plans I thought were surefire. But the salesman says that some of the ladies who look at them think the dining rooms are too small, while others say they are too big. Some don't like air-conditioning and won't pay for something they won't use." He put another spoonful of sugar into his coffee. "Ha, they'll sing a different tune when the thermometer registers a hundred and ten in the shade!"

Grandpa took a thoughtful puff on his old corncob pipe and said sagely, "I thought 'twould be so."

The old man had been given at least a dozen brierwood pipes by his children, but he still preferred one made of a cob.

"Lots of old ways better'n the newfangled ones," he would often say in an attempt to justify his stand.

"Set in his ways," was the way Papa laughingly put it. Papa would say also that his papa had the best hindsight in the country, that the old man could always tell a person what he should have done *after* a mistake had been made.

But Papa was properly respectful to him now.

Then Mama spoke up. "You've had this trouble before, Tate. Some houses have sold slower than others. Besides, the first houses in a new subdivision are always the hardest to sell."

"I know." Papa winked at her and chucked Ricky under the chin. "I just like to borrow trouble, I reckon."

He chuckled then and turned to his mother. "Let's talk about something else. Mama, how's your garden this year?"

Teddi saw Grandma shake her head mournfully, then she fled. As she did she heard, as she had expected, Grandma say sadly, "Trifling, that's what. I declare, my tomato plants are the puniest-looking things. . . ."

Which sounded just like Grandma, Teddi thought as she ran to her room. The old lady could point at the most gorgeous row of vegetables or flowers and declare that they were the sorriest things she had ever seen in her whole life!

Were Papa's worries as baseless as Grandma's statements? Teddi hoped so.

Why did her parents have to be concerned about money now, anyhow? Didn't she have enough to worry about with no one but that smart aleck Jimmy Bryant coming to her pool party?

She went to the window at the side of her room and looked down toward the driveway. Her spirits sank even lower. For there, parked beside one of Papa's new trucks, was Uncle Jobe's old, beaten-up black sedan.

Where was Grandpa's own shiny compact car? Probably being used by one of his six daughters-in-law, or Aunt Daisy, or Aunt Kate, Teddi thought resentfully. One of them was always borrowing it to drive to a P.T.A. meeting or Home Demonstration Club meetings or run some silly errand or other, leaving the old folks whatever old wreck that happened to be handy. Grandma and Grandpa never seemed to mind. But suddenly Teddi minded—very much.

For there, beside the Moore house next door, stood Nancy with a boy about her age, looking over toward the old car and laughing. Teddi couldn't blame them. Uncle Jobe's old car would have been a real attraction at an exhibition of ancient vehicles.

Cheeks burning with embarrassment, Teddi turned away from the window. Nancy Moore would never be friendly with her now.

She threw herself down on her bed. Face in pillow, she lashed her feet up and down in pure frustration. Other people on the Hill might live enchanted lives with no worries or cares, but not Teddi Taylor.

She rolled over and sat up, staring balefully at her toes. She had no friends, either. No friend would have written that note of Jimmy's. And she hadn't heard a thing from Viv or the others.

It was maddening, too. She had so much to show them, the pool and all, and they wouldn't even come to see them.

The telephone tinkled and she let it ring. No sense in answering it. It was probably a call for Papa, anyway.

Mama's voice drifted up to her.

"Teddi," she called softly. "Telephone."

Teddi sat up, dazed. Telephone for her? The possibilities made her jump.

"Thanks, Mama," she called back.

She picked up the small phone from the cradle on her desk. "Hello," she said breathlessly.

A tiny girlish voice whispered into her ear, "Is this Miss Taylor?"

"Miss Taylor? Why, yes, do you mean me?"

"I mean Miss Teddi Taylor who invited me to her pool party."

"That's me. I mean I." Teddi was flustered. It was the first time anyone had called for *Miss* Taylor on the telephone. After this she'd pick up the receiver and say crisply, "Miss Taylor speaking."

Still, that wouldn't do, either. A caller might think it was Mama. In Southern speech Miss and Mrs. often sounded alike.

"Teddi talking." No, that wasn't right.

"Teddi Taylor speaking." Oh, pipes, she'd figure it out later.

"This is Cora," the tiny voice continued. "You know, Cora Walker?"

"Oh, why, yes, Cora, how are you?"

A picture of Cora floated before Teddi. She was a timid,

mousy girl who stammered and blushed when anyone said "hello" to her. She and Teddi had been classmates from kindergarten, but never friends.

It was so easy to overlook Cora. But it wasn't easy to overlook Cora's brother, Jack. He was a junior and just as attractive and popular as Cora was plain and self-conscious. Why, he often dated girls like Tess Graves!

Jack was a catch for any girl giving a party, and Teddi wanted so much for him to come to hers.

But, in asking him, she had known she could not ignore his sister. For, though Jack and Cora had very different personalities, they were devoted to each other.

"Oh, I'm fine," Cora's words tumbled out. "Only I can't come to your party."

Teddi reeled as though struck by a physical blow. This meant that Jack wouldn't come, either. She had especially hoped that he would come. Since receiving Jimmy's smart note, she had been thinking of a plan to put him in his place. And Jack had played an important part in those plans.

Now that she lived on the Hill she was fairly sure that Jack would wake up to the fact that she was alive. He had always been partial to girls from well-to-do families. Though he came from a family of moderate means himself, his good looks and flair had helped him date some of the most socially prominent girls in town.

Right now Teddi managed a weak, "Oh, I'm so sorry."

"Well, so'm I." Cora's voice lifted as though she were pleased at the assurance she would be missed. Then she went on hastily, "My mother and I are going to Nashville Saturday and we won't be back until real late. But," she added as a sort of afterthought, "Jack told me to tell you he'd be there."

At that moment Grandma called from downstairs.

"Thelma! Me 'n' Grampy are going now. Be a good girl."

Teddi slapped her hand over the mouthpiece.

"Bye, Grandma," she called back, her throat so full of elation she almost choked. "I'll try."

Then she lifted her hand and glowed into the phone, "Oh, wonderful!"

"Well, bye."

"Bye."

Teddi fairly danced down the stairs. She went out the back door just in time to see Grandma and Grandpa wave good-bye to Mama and Papa as their old car turned into Holly Tree Lane.

Her gaze was then drawn toward the Moore house. Nancy was still in the backyard. Teddi's spirits flew at full mast. Why not? She waved at Nancy. And Nancy waved back, though quite languidly.

Suddenly feeling very brave, Teddi thought, *I'll just go over and talk to her.*

After all, if Jack Walker was coming to her party, anything was possible.

Should she ask Nancy to come, too? Well, not to this particular party. For, with the exception of Jack, and possibly Jimmy, a sophisticated girl like Nancy would have nothing in common with her old friends. Perhaps later . . . she'd give a party and ask Nancy and Tess and Mimi and. . . .

As she walked toward the Moore house she saw Nancy rise. Then, a few feet from the lawn table with its huge fringed umbrella that threw a shadow over the chaise longue on which the Moore girl had been sitting, she realized it wasn't Nancy at all, but her mother!

They looked so much alike—the same slim figure and blond hair. And they dressed alike in shorts and cotton knit blouses.

Confused, Teddi started to turn. But Mrs. Moore stopped

her with a blithe, "Well, hi. I suppose it is time we became acquainted now that we're neighbors and all."

Teddi stopped, speechless for a moment. Mrs. Moore continued amusedly, "Friends of yours?"

Teddi turned, bewildered. "Who?"

Mrs. Moore laughed, her heavily coated lips leaving a raspberry stain on her small white teeth. Her violet-shadowed eyes twinkled mirthfully.

"Those characters in that old car."

Suddenly Teddi understood. Mrs. Moore was talking about her grandma and grandpa! Shaken and unnerved, she stammered, "Er, ah, no. They're just country folks who leave us fresh eggs and vegetables every week."

6

Flying High

Instantly Teddi recoiled at her own words. But what else could she have said? Told the truth and made herself the object of Mrs. Moore's brittle amusement?

The back door of the Moore house opened. Onto the patio walked Nancy. This time Teddi was sure it was she. There couldn't be three people who looked so much alike.

When Nancy smiled and said, "Hi there, neighbor!" Teddi saw Nancy and her mother were smile-alikes, too.

Teddi found herself almost speechless in the presence of Nancy and the tall, good-looking boy who had come out with her. But she did manage to stammer, "I saw your mama out here and thought it was you."

Nancy raised her hand and brows in mock horror. "Oh, no!" she cried. "Don't call her that! My *mother,* I mean. She says it makes her feel so old."

At Teddi's bewildered look, Nancy grinned impishly and added, "Her name is Alicia, but she likes *Tish* even better."

Unsmiling, Tish ground out her cigarette in an ashtray on the top of a white-enameled table. "Very funny," she said. "Anyway, everyone takes us for sisters. Why disillusion them?"

53

The tall, dark boy started to say something. Then, seeming to think better of it, he turned and gave Teddi a friendly grin. Though his teeth were a bit too prominent, he was a very handsome boy. In well-cut continental slacks, he was the perfect picture of the kind of young man Teddi had expected to find in the homes on the Hill.

She was glad then that Mama hadn't noticed she was wearing one of her best summer cottons, a pale yellow sheer with schiffli embroidery, though she was uncomfortably aware that such a dress was not proper for morning wear on the Hill. Nancy and Tish wore shorts and sleeveless blouses.

If the boy noticed anything amiss in her dress, he gave no sign.

"Since no one is going to introduce me," he bantered, "I'll do it myself. I'm Eddie Thomas."

Nancy laughed, easily. Teddi wished she could be like her —poised and unflustered.

"You'll have to excuse me," Nancy said, with no trace of apology in her voice. "Eddie is just back from prep school and I'm not accustomed to having him around yet."

Teddi was more awestruck than ever. Here she was, Teddi Taylor, lately come from Colfax Street, hobnobbing with a girl from a private academy and a boy from prep school! What would the old gang think if they could see her now?

They were likely to say that she was flying pretty high.

Still there was no reason for her to feel a bit inferior in the presence of Nancy and Tish and Eddie, she thought fiercely. Wasn't her house as big and imposing as the Moores'? Or the Thomases'? She had heard Papa say that a family named Thomas lived in the big, turreted, Victorian-styled house three doors down the street. And she assumed Eddie belonged to that family.

Nancy brought her back to the present. "I guess we don't know your name."

"Teddi. Teddi Taylor."

"How attractive. Suits you, too."

"Oh, come now!" Tish broke in. "Let's not get gushy." She turned to Eddie. "How about some tennis? Nan, be a dear, and get a couple of racquets."

"I'll get them," Eddie said quickly. He turned to Teddi. "How about doubles? You play, don't you?"

Before she had time to reply, Teddi heard a door slam. She knew it was the back door of her own house. Papa came striding toward the truck with TAYLOR CONSTRUCTION COMPANY printed in big letters on the door of its cab.

Teddi was humiliated. Papa was dressed in his workday outfit of faded wash trousers and shirt and heavy, thick-soled shoes. He looked exactly like a member of the construction crew.

What a contrast to Mr. Moore, whom she had seen leaving the house every morning wearing a dark business suit with white shirt and four-in-hand tie and polished shoes! She was certain Eddie's father dressed the same.

She hoped that Nancy and Tish and Eddie would think that Papa was a part of a crew of the Taylor Construction Company. But that hope was soon shattered by Papa's calling to her, "I'm going over to the old place, hon. Wanta get Rick and go along?"

He waved jovially at the others and they waved back. Then Tish said with undisguised relief, "Well, that settles that!"

Teddi muttered good-bye, turned, and fled back toward home.

What good was it, she thought, to have a fine home in an exclusive neighborhood if you didn't have a family to go with it? What an opportunity she had had to become friendly with Nancy and Tish and Eddie! And Papa had come along and spoiled it.

"Better hustle, honey." Papa grinned at her, unaware that he had just shattered her bright future. "I'm in a hurry."

You're always in a hurry, Teddi thought in disgust. But she didn't say it. If there was one thing Papa couldn't stand, he had often said, it was impertinent children.

Mama was in the living room dusting when she went in search of Ricky.

"I've some cleaning to do upstairs, Teddi." She smiled as she patted Rick on top of his blond curls and sent him toddling toward his sister. "I musn't let work pile up for Elvira on her day off. While Rick is a dandy little helper, I think I can get things done faster alone."

Papa had suggested this little excursion for that very reason, Teddi thought resentfully. She bet the other ladies on the Hill didn't do any of their housework or make baby-sitters of their daughters.

The sight of Ricky's unsteady approach put her resentment to flight, however. She kneeled and smiled encouragement at her baby brother. Reaching her, he fell triumphantly into her arms. She kissed his fat, wrinkled neck.

"Keep your eye on him every minute," Mama warned, plumping a cushion on the rose-colored sofa. "You know how fast he can get away."

Teddi rose, holding Rick by one plump hand.

"Yes'm, I know," she replied, smiling down at him. He looked up and cooed, "Go-bye."

"Go-bye, you bet."

"Go-bye-bet," he mimicked her happily.

He toddled beside her down the hall and out the back door,

still chattering. Measuring her steps to match his, she tried to understand what he was saying so she could talk back to him.

"Hey, big boy!" Papa cried at sight of him. He picked up his youngest son and plumped him onto the seat of the truck. Then he surprised Teddi by putting his hands about her waist and lifting her up beside Ricky.

"I can get up by myself, Papa," she giggled.

"I know you can," he replied, circling the front of the truck and climbing up behind the wheel. "But I wanted you up here right quick before Big Boy tried running away with my rig."

"Biboy!" cried Ricky, beaming.

Papa grinned down at Rick, at the same time turning the wheel with quick, decisive movements of his big hands. As they whirled about, Teddi saw Nancy sitting alone on the patio next door. Tish and Eddie were engaged in a strenuous game of tennis on the clay court nearby.

It was then she realized something she hadn't thought about before. There was no swimming pool in the Moore backyard!

A few minutes later she sat up straight. "I thought we were going to the old house on Colfax Street," she said.

Without looking at her, Papa replied, "Decided I'd run out to Mountainside first."

His voice, she noticed, had lost its jolly ring. *He really is worried about those houses out there,* she thought.

"Is there really a chance we will go to the poorhouse, Papa?" she asked, in what she hoped was a joking way.

Papa turned and gave her a quizzical look as he slowed down for changing lights. Frowning slightly, he asked, "Now what made you ask that?"

"Well, I heard you tell Mama and Grandma and Grandpa that we might go there."

"Po'house!" Ricky squealed belatedly.

Papa grinned fondly at both of them and patted Ricky's hand.

"Think nothing of it. That's just my way of talking," he said. But he didn't reassure her much when he added, "We can always go back to the house on Colfax Street. I haven't sold it yet, and it's paid for and clear."

But I don't want to go back! Teddi thought in panic. She had had a taste of flying high and she liked it.

Soon they passed between two stone gateposts. Standing one on each side of a newly paved road, they bore bronze plates that read MOUNTAINSIDE ESTATES.

A short time later they stopped before one of two big houses built side by side. Small, bright-colored pennants fluttered from wires strung from the corners of the roofs. In the newly seeded yards were FOR SALE and OPEN HOUSE signs. A salesman sat on the cement stoop of one of the houses, waiting for customers.

"That ad drawing?" Papa yelled at him.

"Not yet, Tate," came back the reply.

Papa shook his head. "Well, stick to it," he said, and they were off again in a whirl of red dust.

They stopped again before another house under construction. Mr. Newby, the foreman, came out and stuck his head in the cab of the truck.

"Hi there, blockbuster," he grinned at Ricky. Then he turned to Teddi. "How's come we don't see you around anymore?" he inquired. "Carol was sayin' at the supper table last evenin' that she hadn't seen you in a coon's age."

Teddi almost replied that Carol hadn't said she was coming to her pool party. But Papa spoke up for her. "We're going over that way right now," he said. "Want to check on those painters decorating the house. The renters will be here soon and I want it ready for them."

Then he and Mr. Newby talked for a few minutes about the progress on the unfinished house. Workmen appeared from time to time, carrying lumber or saws or pieces of sheetrock.

Papa waved and yelled at each one, calling him Joe or Tom or Les, and asking how he was and if his family was all right.

Papa would never change, Teddi thought mournfully. His humble beginnings would always show no matter how rich he became or to what part of the town he moved. And he would never *try* to be different, either.

Soon they were on their way again. Approaching the old neighborhood, the streets and houses became increasingly familiar. Then they rounded the corner of Colfax and Main where sat the long, low building whose Coca Cola sign hanging in front proclaimed it to be BRYANT'S GROCERY.

Teddi didn't see Jimmy and she was glad of it. Mr. Bryant, however, looked out of the window just as they passed the store. He waved happily.

Papa waved back and hollered, "Mornin', Mr. Bryant. How's the family?"

"Fine. And yours?"

"Fine."

On they went. They passed Ruby Hart's home, an old sagging house with four chimneys and a stone foundation, set back on a scraggly lawn. A sleeping dog lay beside two old tires which Teddi knew were playthings of Ruby's small brother and sister. Papers were scattered all over the place, and here and there she even saw a tin can.

"That yard could stand some cleaning," Papa commented, reading her thoughts. "But Mrs. Hart, being a widow and clerking downtown all day, has little time for anything like that, I suppose."

And Teddi knew that Ruby was busier than most teen-agers, helping with the housework and caring for the other children. But that yard certainly didn't help the looks of the neighborhood, though she hadn't noticed its bedraggled appearance so much when she had lived there.

Across the street was the Newby bungalow. It was freshly painted and the yard had just been mowed and the shrubs and hedge trimmed. The red rambler roses, of which Mrs. Newby was so proud, flaunted their beauty from a trellis alongside.

But how tiny the house was. It seemed to have shrunken to the size of a dollhouse since she had moved away.

And the Robinson house! She had thought it so stately when she had spent half her time there with Viv. Now it looked like what it really was: a big, old frame house with a wide porch on three sides. A porch swing hung behind a flowering vine with several splint-bottomed rockers scattered about. Huge pots of petunias and trailing vines sat on the tops of the square posts beside the steps. A fiber rug ran back to the screen door.

Old Red, Viv's Irish setter, was sprawled in his usual place before the door. He never seemed to learn that this was the wrong place for him to rest, since he had to move every time anybody went in or out. But he usually received a pat on the head at such times, so perhaps he thought it was worth the effort, Teddi thought reflectively.

"Well, here we are!" Papa cried, swinging the truck into the gravel driveway of their old home.

He lifted Rick out of the cab and helped Teddi down. Teddi stared about her in disbelief. Had she ever lived in this awful place?

The house, which she had once thought so pretty, now looked as old and drab as any on the street. It was covered with imitation-brick siding, and rooms had been added to the original structure with no thought of architectural beauty. Papa had put a big picture window where none should have been. Mama had added a many-windowed solarium on the other side. A concrete stoop in front was edged with a black, ornamental iron railing, the posts of which groped their way up to its metal-canopied roof.

Teddi closed her eyes. She hoped fervently that neither Nancy nor Mimi nor Tish nor Eddie ever found out that she had lived *here* before moving to the Hill.

A wild desire seized her to get out of this awful neighborhood—and its associations—just as soon as she could.

At that instant she heard a side door of the Robinson house open and slam shut. Then Viv appeared on the porch. Quickly Teddi pulled Ricky beside her and crouched behind the truck.

She had absolutely nothing she wanted to say to Viv!

She hoped fervently that Viv hadn't seen her. She quieted Ricky so Viv couldn't hear his protests at being pulled to the ground. The few seconds she waited there seemed like an hour. Then she heard the door slam again. A sigh of relief escaped her. She peeked around the corner of the bed of the truck, sweeping the side porch with her gaze until she was certain that Viv had gone back into the house.

7

Clean Break

"Coming in?" Papa called from the front stoop where he had just unlocked the door.

"Yes, Papa!" The words burst thankfully from Teddi as she ran toward the opening door to escape any further chance of Viv's seeing her.

But a tiny flame of guilt flared within her. Hadn't she criticized Viv for not calling and accepting her invitation to the pool party? Now she had seen her best friend and hadn't even spoken to her.

"You'll change." Jimmy's words came back, mocking her. She had changed, she guessed, for she never would have done such a thing before.

Holding tightly to Ricky's hand, she stepped inside the familiar hallway. Her mind sought to spin a web on which to hang her feelings of guilt. Papa should never have brought her here. Nothing good could come from returning to old haunts. All it did was revive old memories and associations that should be forgotten.

When making a break, it was best to make it clean.

She looked around the interior of the house that had been

her home for so long. How shabby it looked in comparison to the new house on the Hill!

"I'll never come back here again," she told herself firmly.

From now on she would stay in her new world, where everything was big and bright and elegant. Though she had no friends there now, she soon would have, she was sure. From now on all her efforts would be directed toward becoming friendly with Nancy and Tess and Eddie and Mimi Martineaux. She'd manage it, too, in spite of her family.

The clomping of Papa's shoes on the bare floors echoed through the empty house. Although her mind was elsewhere, she could follow his tour through the rooms.

When the pool party was over she would break all ties with her old friends on Colfax Street. The fewer of them that came to her party the better. It would mean fewer ties to break.

Mr. Taylor came back down the stairs. Heading back toward the kitchen, he grumbled, "Those painters and paperhangers haven't been here yet."

Teddi stepped into the large room off the hallway that Grandma Taylor called the parlor. How forlorn and shabby it looked now. Bright spots on the faded wallpaper showed plainly where pictures had hung. Dark streaks told where the backs of chairs and sofas had scraped.

"The sofa Papa gave to the Newbys sat right over there," Teddi mused. "And at each end was a pine lamp table Dave had made in woodworking class at junior high."

Those same tables were now in the family room of their new house, for Mama had refused to part with them. The interior decorator Papa had hired to furnish the house had called them "quaintly primitive" and said they would look fairly well there.

Teddi turned slowly and regarded another side of the room. There, before the big window, had sat the tall, spreading fern that Mama had mourned when the decorator had said it simply would not fit *anywhere* in their new house. Teddi remembered with affection the old chair that had sat beside it—and how everybody had dived for that particular comfortable spot from which to view the television set opposite it.

Turning again, she faced the old-fashioned fireplace with a railing around the hearth. Two platform rockers had sat facing it, favorites of both her grandmas. There the old ladies had rested after helping Elvira wash dishes following big family dinners.

Memories flooded back—happy memories of cousins, aunts, uncles, and grandparents everywhere. Would they ever have such family gatherings in the house on the Hill?

Uncle Jobe, one of Papa's brothers, had once said before they had moved that he would feel like a fish out of water up there among all those fancy folks. So far neither he nor Aunt Lil nor any of their children had visited them. Of all their relatives in Redwing Crossing, only her grandparents had come to the new house on the Hill.

Her words to Tish flashed back to her. What would Papa say if he learned she had called *his* mama and papa country folks who brought them fresh vegetables and eggs?

She felt trapped in the mesh of her own words. Her eyes again took in the homely interior of the old house. A lump formed in her throat. She had never felt ashamed of any of her relatives while living here.

Some things about living on the Hill were not so pleasant, she decided. Living up to the standards of the neighbors was one of them.

She was so lost in thought that she did not notice Ricky's

hand slipping out of hers. Racing upstairs, she stopped misty-eyed in the doorway of her old room. All the well-loved pieces of furniture that had been there seemed to float back into their places. There was her pretty maple bed. How many happy times she and Viv had lain across it, talking and reading and giggling.

She whirled and looked down the upstairs hall, at the end of which was the huge room shared by her parents. Door ajar, it looked just as it did on the many Christmas mornings when she and Dave and Dixie had barged into it.

There, through the doorway on the left, was Dixie's room. What a mess it had always been! Lead, bronze, and porcelain figures of animals had been everywhere. The walls had been covered with pictures of dogs, cats, horses, and cows that Dixie had cut out of magazines.

Beyond it was Dave's room and across the hall was the room that had been a sort of nursery for each of them, from Dave right down to Rick.

Rick? She turned, startled. Where was Rick? She raced quickly downstairs, through the dining room and into the kitchen.

"Papa," she panted. "Have you seen Rick?"

"Not since I saw him with you about five minutes ago."

"Oh, dear, where could he be now?"

"Almost anywhere. And you'd better run him down."

Teddi ran back toward the front door. There she almost collided with Jimmy, coming through it with Rick in tow.

At sight of both of them her heart gave a jump.

"Say, does this little stray belong to you?" Jimmy grinned. With a sweeping gesture, he indicated Rick. "He was headed for the store when I picked him up."

"Po' house," Ricky beamed.

Teddi, relieved, smiled a warm welcome at both of them. Then she pursed her lips and responded to Jimmy's banter.

"Seems to me he did come here with us," she said, tapping a foot and looking up at the ceiling. "Or did he?"

"He looks like a little feller that used to live here. I saw your dad's truck in the driveway and just thought I'd ask."

Both began to laugh. Then Jimmy sobered a bit to add, "Seems like old times, finding you folks here."

"Seems like old times being here."

Mr. Taylor appeared then. He grinned at the sight of them.

"Well, I see you found my boy," he said. "Teddi, for the next couple of hours I would advise you to put him on a chain and hang the chain around your neck. I've got to run out to the brickyard and see about delivery of the bricks for that new house in Mountainside. I'll be back for you as soon as I'm through."

He shooed them out of the house and locked the door behind him. As he walked toward the truck he jerked a thumb toward the Robinson house. "Viv is home. I saw her a minute ago." And with a wave of his hand he backed the truck out of the driveway and was off down Colfax Street.

Teddi stood bewildered. What was she going to do for the next two hours? Papa didn't know, of course, that she and Viv weren't on speaking terms. And Carol and Ruby might not even be home.

Faintly she heard Jimmy say, "Viv sure will be glad to see you."

"Oh, no, she won't," Teddi almost replied.

Viv had probably seen her hiding behind the truck and had guessed why she was there. In spite of her misgivings, however, she found herself, with Jimmy beside her, headed for the Robinson house.

Big Red approached them, his plume of a tail waving a welcome. Teddi stopped to pat him on the head, while Ricky hugged the big dog around the neck.

Viv answered their knock. At sight of Teddi her eyes popped. Hands pressed to forehead, she staggered backward. Then she came back close to the screen and peered through. She shook her head, muttering, "It is! Believe it or not, it is Teddi Taylor, my old sidekick."

Teddi giggled, relieved. If Viv had seen her hiding behind the truck, she was doing a good job of hiding any resentment she might feel.

"Oh, can the corny dramatics," Teddi laughed gaily. "It's me."

Viv ignored that remark to take a few purposely wobbly steps.

"Gosh, for a minute I thought I'd seen a ghost!"

Then she, too, burst out laughing and opened the door. "I saw your dad's truck over there but I didn't know you were with him. Come in, come in."

Teddi, Jimmy, and Rick stepped eagerly into the darkened house. Teddi took a few stumbling steps before her eyes became adjusted to the lack of light. All the shades were drawn against the hot rays of the sun. Windows and doors were closed to keep in the cool air drawn in by window fans during the night.

For a moment it seemed strange to Teddi to be in a house that wasn't air-conditioned. But the feeling soon passed and the old way of keeping a house cool in summer seemed very natural.

Viv led them to the kitchen. Mrs. Robinson, a tall, spare woman with graying hair, turned from the oven from which she had just taken a pan of cupcakes. Other cakes, white and dark, some frosted and some not, lay on clean towels on the counter tops.

"Well, look who's here!" she cried. She set down the pan on a hot pad. "Teddi Taylor, as I live and breathe. How are you, Teddi? And your mama?" Her eyes twinkling, she wiped her floury hands on her apron. "And there's my sweetie pie, Rick, bless his heart!"

She grabbed a startled Ricky, lifted him, and kissed him soundly on a cheek. Ricky wriggled mightily to free himself from her embrace. Succeeding, he darted for the back door.

Mrs. Robinson picked up one of the frosted cupcakes and coaxed him back.

"One won't hurt him," she said, looking at Teddi. "I do recollect how particular your mama was about her young 'uns not eating sweets between meals."

"Wish you'd been as strict with me, Mama," Viv grinned, picking up frosted cupcakes for Teddi and Jimmy and herself. "If you had, maybe I wouldn't be so fat now."

Her mother laughed. "Sweets for the sweet, I always say. And how could I know you'd take after your papa's side of the family?" she countered. "And not mine. We stay as skinny as beanstalks no matter what, or how much, we eat."

Jimmy winked at Teddi. "Viv's not really fat, is she?"

"I don't think so."

"Well, thank you!" Viv cried, and she gave each of them another cupcake. Then, her eyes on Teddi, she pointed to some unfrosted cakes. "Wanta help frost?"

"Oh, yes."

The direction of Viv's pointed finger switched to two bowls of frosting.

"Light or dark?"

"Umm. Dark."

Teddi settled herself on a kitchen stool beside the counter and began to swirl the thick brown sweetness onto the light-as-feather cakes.

Just like old times, she thought. She wondered how many such sessions she had spent in the Robinson kitchen, talking and frosting something delicious that Mrs. Robinson was constantly baking.

And eating, too, just as they were doing now. Like all good cooks, Mrs. Robinson liked to see the products of her efforts enjoyed. And enjoyed they were; she saw to that, by passing them out freely to visitors and neighbors as well as to her family.

"Next best thing to living beside a free bakery," Mr. Taylor always said.

While Teddi helped Viv frost cakes, Jimmy played with Rick, and Big Red looked wistfully through the screen door, they chattered about a variety of things.

Suddenly the subject of the pool party came up.

"Boy, that should be fun!" Viv cried with her usual enthusiasm. All the cakes now frosted, she put the empty frosting bowl under a faucet and sent steaming water into it. "It will be worth all the effort Carol and Ruby and I have put into getting ready for it."

Teddi turned to her in surprise.

"What do you mean, getting ready for it?"

Viv's flushed face puckered soberly. "Just what I said." She turned to Teddi and grinned. "You should have seen the panic that invitation of yours sent us into!" She squirted liquid detergent into the bowl and scrubbed it vigorously with a brush. "None of us had a thing to wear to a party like that."

"But you have a swimsuit," Teddi protested. "And so do the other girls."

Viv rinsed out the bowl with more hot water and reached for a towel. Then she gave Teddi a withering look. "Do you really think we'd wear those old rags to a party on the Hill? Well, I should say not." She polished the bowl thoroughly. "So we decided to wait until we had the proper outfits for such an affair before we told you whether or not we'd come."

Teddi gulped. So that had been the reason she hadn't heard from them!

"You are coming, aren't you?" she asked anxiously.

"Yep!" Viv cried happily. "You see, we've been baby-sitting, washing windows, house cleaning and all sorts of things to earn money for new suits and a blouse or so. I was going to call you today and tell you we'd be there."

Viv placed the clean bowl on a shelf above the sink.

"Want to see my new suit?" she asked.

"I'd love to."

Viv ran out of the kitchen, untying the strings of her apron as she went. When she returned she held before her a beautiful swimming suit, deep red in color and simply cut. It would be striking with her dark eyes and hair and olive skin, Teddi thought to herself.

Viv smiled at the looks of approval in the eyes of Teddi and Jimmy. "Wait until you see Ruby's," she said. "It's pale blue and she has a cap with rubber cornflowers all over it." Her eyes sparkled. "And Carol's is pale yellow. Mmmm."

Jimmy's grin turned to a frown.

"S'pose I can come in my old trunks? I didn't get any new ones for the party. And I don't think Lyle or Terry did, either."

"Fellows are lucky that way," Viv said. "All they have to do is bring their handsome selves. Nobody thinks a thing about what they wear." She sighed. "But with us girls it's different. It takes a lot of effort for us to get ready for a lot of fun."

Then she whirled about and fairly danced out of the room. Teddi watched her go, thinking how lucky she was to have friends like Viv and Ruby and Carol. Being with them one could almost forget their shabby surroundings. Shabby? She looked out the window overlooking the Robinson backyard and wondered how she could ever, even for a second, have thought the neighborhood looked shabby. The green lawn was well tended, as was a small vegetable garden at the rear. The limbs of a beautiful big maple tree spread benevolently across one side of the yard and extended over into the backyard of her own old home.

The old house looks beautiful, she thought to herself. *Just as nice as when I lived there and was so proud of it.*

"It's awfully nice to be back," she whispered—to nobody in particular.

At that moment she felt arms about her waist and was startled when Jimmy planted a gentle kiss on her cheek.

"That's for not changing," he whispered, "just as I hoped you wouldn't."

Then, hearing Mrs. Robinson coming from the pantry, he stepped quickly away from her and began to study intently a potted geranium in the window.

Teddi blushed furiously. She should be indignant, she supposed. But she wasn't. Instead she rubbed her cheek softly with the palm of her hand.

Suddenly Papa's voice came from the direction of the back door.

"I declare this is the best smelling kitchen I've been in since I left home this morning," he cried, sniffing deeply.

Panic struck Teddi. Had Papa seen Jimmy kissing her? If he had, he gave no sign.

"Come in, Tate," Mrs. Robinson said heartily. She pointed

to the frosted cupcakes. "Have one."

"Don't mind if I do," Papa said. He frowned at the cakes. "Which kind should I take, light or dark?"

Viv reappeared. "Take one of each, Mr. Taylor," she said.

"I was hoping somebody would say that."

He took two and ate them with relish, taking a bite of one and then the other.

Mrs. Robinson fairly beamed.

"I declare," she said, "we certainly have missed you folks since you moved away. I do hope you will come back soon."

She and Viv and Jimmy walked with them out to the truck.

"We'll be back soon," Mr. Taylor promised. "Won't we, Teddi?"

"We certainly will," Teddi replied fervently.

8

Homespun Hours

As Papa's truck made its slow way up the Hill, Teddi felt a change come over her. Faint at first, it grew stronger with each palatial home they passed. When they turned into the driveway of the Taylor home, she wondered how she could have felt, even for a short while, at home on Colfax Street. She wondered, too, what she had had in common with Mrs. Robinson, Viv, and Jimmy.

Her new life was very different from the old! Once in her lovely room, the realization hit her full force. *I'm like a chameleon, I guess,* she mused as she gazed around at its spaciousness and expensive furnishings. *My color changes with my surroundings.*

She would never go back to Colfax Street. The homespun hours she had spent there should be forgotten. Her home was on the Hill now. She was no longer Teddy Taylor whose father was a building contractor. Instead she was Teddi Taylor, daughter of the head of a prosperous construction company. From now on she would live the part.

She sat down in a chair before her mirror and practiced a sort of languid, sophisticated, bored-with-it-all attitude. This

Teddi could never enjoy frosting cupcakes and chatting in the kitchen!

"Hurry, Teddi!" Mama's voice coming from downstairs put a sudden end to her practice. "Lunch is ready and Papa is in a hurry to get back to work."

Papa and his hurrying! He seemed to put his work ahead of everything. She sighed. Her only problem now was her family.

Well, she wasn't going to hurry. She didn't, either, until Dave yelled, "For gosh sakes, get a move on! I'm starved."

She eyed the meal with disapproval when she entered the dining room. The food Mama had prepared was very good, as usual. But it should have been served by a maid, not put on the table all at once.

Teddi sat very properly, hands folded in her lap, and looked around the table. This was the way meals were served on Colfax Street, she thought as the dishes were passed around and everyone served himself.

"All my favorite foods," Papa remarked contentedly as he helped himself to the meat-loaf ring piled high in the center with fluffy mashed potatoes and dribbled with golden brown gravy. Then, on the same plate, he put salad, green beans, fried okra, and a cornmeal muffin.

He did not seem to realize his daughter's eyes were on him, regarding him unhappily.

When Mama asked about the old neighbors, Papa laughed, wrinkling deeply at the corners of his eyes.

"I reckon Teddi can tell you more about them than I can," he chuckled, his muscular shoulders shaking. "She seemed to be getting along uncommonly well with one of them, anyhow."

Teddi picked at her own meat loaf, her cheeks burning. Papa had seen Jimmy kissing her! Resentment against Jimmy flared within her. What an embarrassing position he had put her into! Well, she'd see to it that he never had a chance to do so again. After lunch, she'd call him and put him in his place. She had two accounts to settle with him—the kissing and his smart-aleck note.

Still, perhaps she shouldn't do that, either. She had to think of the pool party. After all the preparations Viv and Carol and Ruby had made, she mustn't spoil it for them. It would probably be the biggest thing in their lives. And besides, she wanted them to see the new house and the pool.

She felt all eyes on her and realized she had to say something.

"Everybody I saw was fine, Mama," she said hastily. "Mrs. Robinson asked how you were. We frosted cupcakes and talked."

"Cupcakes!" Ricky said clearly.

"Did you hear that?" Papa exclaimed. "He's talking real plain."

The whole family gave Ricky fondly admiring looks. He was a remarkable child!

"What did you talk about?" Mama asked at last.

"Oh, Viv told me about one of her cousins from River Junction who is going to college this fall. She seemed to think it was something wonderful."

Papa generously buttered a muffin.

"Well, it is wonderful," he said, taking a bite. His blue eyes looked around at his family. "And it is something I've promised myself that I'm going to give my children. They're going to college."

After a second's pause he added, as an afterthought, "I didn't have the chance to go myself and I've always regretted it."

He continued to talk about how much a college education can mean to the young folks of today. He remembered when

Dave had talked briefly of dropping out of high school and going to work.

"Today's jobs demand skilled people," he had said over and over. "A college degree is an absolute necessity."

"You don't have one," Dave had countered.

"I grew up in different times," Papa had replied. "When I was a boy there were still jobs for unskilled workers. But machines have taken over most of those."

Teddi listened with half an ear as Papa went over the same conversation again. She was glad he had temporarily forgotten the kiss he must have observed through the Robinsons' back door.

Actually she thought the prospect of going to college was wonderful, too. It was another thing that set her apart from the other girls in the old gang. She was the only one of them who could casually say, "When I go to college. . . ."

It sounded positively glamorous. It would mean becoming pledged to a sorority and having her picture in the hometown paper with a write-up about it.

She and Viv and Ruby and Carol would be even farther apart then. The best Viv could do would be to take a course at the local business school, where there was absolutely no social life. After that she would work in an office until she married Lyle or some other Holston boy. They would live in the same neighborhood as her parents. Nothing would change for Viv—nothing at all.

Ruby's mother wouldn't even be able to send her to a business school. And Carol wouldn't even want to go; she disliked school of any kind. Both girls would start working as soon as they finished high school.

Of course, all that would mean nothing to Teddi. By that time she would be associating only with girls like Mimi and

Tess and Nancy and others like them whom she would be meeting soon.

She heard Dave's rueful chuckle. "Boy, am I glad I stayed in school and now have the chance to go to college! This job I have on the construction crew this summer has made me realize that swinging a pickax is not the easiest way of making a living, even if a machine never takes it over. I don't want to spend the rest of my life doing it."

Teddi looked up, certain that what Dave was really saying was that he didn't like working with the members of such a crew. He was changing his attitude, as she was, toward things that he had once accepted without question.

Dixie broke into the conversation with a blunt, "How come the Moore twins can keep a dog on their property and I can't have Cottonblossom here?"

"Because dogs don't baa," Teddi said with a touch of hauteur. Honestly, with Papa's truck in the driveway, and his work clothes, and grandparents coming and going, the Taylors didn't need a goat to make the neighbors raise their eyebrows!

Dixie drank deeply of her iced tea, at the same time eyeing her sister balefully. Setting down the glass she answered, "Maybe not, but they sure do a good job of barking."

Teddi tossed her head. "A shed would look great by the pool."

"The Moores have a doghouse by their patio."

"Oh, you're hopeless."

After the meal Teddi and Dixie cleared the table and readied the kitchen for Elvira's return. They were very careful to set everything in place for Elvira had very definite ideas about the order of *her* kitchen when she came back from her day off. She wanted it just as she had left it.

As they were finishing, Mama came down and said that

she and Rick were going to spend the afternoon with Grandma Martin.

"Would you girls like to come along?" she asked.

"I would!" Dixie cried happily. "I want to see old Tam's new kittens."

Teddi took the last clean glass from the dishwasher and placed it on a shelf above the sink.

"I think I'll stay home and read," she said. Grandma Martin lived in a neighborhood of modest homes, a neighborhood like their old one. Teddi had had all the Colfax Streets she wanted for one day.

After they left she wandered into the living room. Here she belonged, she felt. It was a decorator's dream come true; it looked like the cover illustration on a *Beautiful Homes* magazine.

Viv would be uneasy in a room like this, just as Teddi would be now on Colfax Street. Still, she hadn't felt out of place there this morning. Teddi rose hastily from a satin-covered wing chair. Life could be so confusing.

It's because I'm alone here, she thought to herself.

What she needed was a close friend who lived on the Hill. Someone who would feel at ease in a room like this.

She wandered out onto the portico and sat down. Would there be any acceptances to her party in the mail today? The party didn't seem important to her now, however. Viv and Ruby and Carol and the others might think it was something to get excited about. But she could hardly wait until it was over.

Suddenly she jumped up. There, coming down the walk on the other side of the street, was Mimi Martineaux! Arms full of books, the tall girl was obviously on her way to the library to exchange them again.

Teddi had completely forgotten the rebuff Mimi had handed her a few days before. And, moreover, she wanted so much to make a friend of Mimi that she would have forgiven the granddaughter of Mrs. Pierre Martineaux for almost anything she might have done.

She ran back into the house and up the stairs, taking the steps two at a time. Two library books which she had just finished reading the night before lay on her desk. She grabbed them up and dashed back down the stairs and out the door to the walk that led down the Hill.

Out on the walk she slowed her pace, making no effort to overtake Mimi. The meeting must look unplanned. Surely somewhere between here and their return home an opportunity would come for them to become acquainted.

Reaching the library, she went in and laid her two books on the desk. Miss Milton, who presided there, smiled a welcome. Then Teddi went toward the shelves featuring the latest in teen-age fiction.

She hoped to find another book by her favorite author, Beverly Brian. This would take luck, however, for Brian books were checked out as fast as they came in. She had tried for weeks to get her latest volume, *Winds of Summer*. She would be content, though, to find one of the other Brian books she had not read.

She looked carefully up and down the shelves. Not one Brian book could she find. She didn't see Mimi, either, though she kept flicking her gaze about in search of her.

Disappointment welled up within her. How she had wanted another Brian book and the chance to chat with Mimi. She was about to take a book by another author when her eyes lit up with delight. There, on a nearby reading table, lay a copy of *Winds of Summer!*

Quickly she walked toward it and picked it up.

"Sorry," said a quiet, though firm, voice from behind her. "That is my book."

Teddi whirled. An unsmiling Mimi Martineaux stood facing her, not a spark of recognition on her long, rather bony face.

Temporarily dazed, Teddi handed over the book. She saw Mimi slap it on top of three other Brian books, turn, and walk toward the check-out desk.

Teddi slowly came back to reality. Of all the nerve. Angrily she grabbed two books by Rosalyn Rogers. She had never read a Rogers book, but that didn't matter to her now.

She followed Mimi back up the Hill, hoping the girl could see that she was being careful this time to keep a few feet behind. She wouldn't speak to her now if Mimi turned and begged her to be her friend.

Anyway, just wait until Saturday night. Her old friends would come to her party and they would have a wonderful time. She'd see Jimmy again, too. Jimmy and Viv! They could make any party hum—he with his guitar and songs, and she with her lively chatter.

Who needed Mimi Martineaux? Teddi turned determinedly into the walk that led to her house without so much as another glance at the tall girl.

In front of the garage beside the house she saw Dave with a strange boy weaving in and out beneath the basketball hoop on the door above. That came as no surprise. Dave often brought friends home with him.

But why wasn't Dave working this afternoon? He had left with Papa in the truck that was now parked on the driveway, far enough back not to interfere with their game.

She shrugged away the question and went on into the house. Inside the door the afternoon mail was neatly stacked on a refectory table. Riffling through it, she flipped out seven envelopes addressed to Miss Teddi Taylor. Eagerly she opened them. To her joy they were all acceptances to her party. Oh, it was going to be a marvelous evening!

Upstairs she went into her room and lay the notes on her desk. Then she happily kicked off her flats and flopped across the bed. Soon she was lost in the story of a girl her own age who had been captured by Indians. This was a wonderful book! How could she have overlooked the Rogers books for so long?

Pages later she rolled over and sat up on the edge of her bed. A Coke would taste good right now. Absentmindedly she poked her feet into some shoes and started for the refrigerator in the kitchen.

Scarcely had she reached the doorway of her room when the telephone on her desk tinkled. She went back and picked up the receiver.

"Teddi Taylor speaking," she said crisply.

"You mean Miss Tedd-eye?" The familiar voice was bantering, yet tender, too.

Her heart seemed to flip right into her throat.

"Why, Jimmy," she said in a choked voice, "it's you."

"Expecting somebody else to call?"

"No, of course not. I mean, it's just that I wasn't expecting a call from you . . . so soon after seeing you, that is. . . ."

"Well, what I'm going to tell you came up sort of suddenly. First, though, I wanted to ask you if you will go to a dance at the Rec Hall a week from Friday night. With me and the others, that is."

"Certainly, I will!" Teddi replied happily.

"Good. Now if my plans turn out right. . . . Say, if I tell you something else, will you promise not to get mad at me?"

"Why, Jimmy, what makes you think I would do that?"

"Well, er, ah, what I'm going to tell you, I guess. And, believe me, I never was so sorry about anything in my whole life, but that's the way things are, I guess."

"What *are* you talking about?" Teddi asked curiously.

"I can't come to your party Saturday night!"

Teddi gasped. Then, for one fleeting second, she was speechless. Then she cried, "And why not?"

"Well, you see, the boys and I . . . you know, the trio—"

The cold wind of anger iced her words. "I suppose you have some old engagement or other?"

"Well, sort of. . . . I wish I could tell you all about it, but I can't. Anyway, you'll be mighty surprised when you find out. . . ."

"I'm sure I will," she replied bitterly. Suddenly she realized she had been tricked into promising that she would go to the dance. Well, he wasn't going to get away with anything like that. "Well, if you can't come to my party, Jimmy Bryant," she snapped, "then I can't go to the dance with you a week from Friday night!" She slammed down the receiver.

"Tsk, tsk." Dixie stuck her head through the doorway of her room. "Such a temper."

"Oh, get lost, will you?"

9

Change of Heart

Dixie didn't get lost. Instead, she stood grinning while Teddi flounced past her and down the stairs.

Teddi didn't feel the way she tried to look, however. Her disappointment in Jimmy was deep. She had always thought she could depend on him. She had been able to forgive him for that smart note he had written; he often teased, and she was accustomed to that—Papa and Dave never let an opportunity pass to do the same. But this was different. Jimmy had broken a promise without giving her a good reason.

An engagement for that silly trio was not a good reason. His thinking so just proved he thought more of them than of her. She sighed. The only way to avoid being hurt by a boy was not to think more of one than another. Well, from now on she wouldn't think much of any of them!

Reaching the bottom of the stairs, she heard the soft slam of the refrigerator door closing. It was followed by the clinking of bottles and the pop of caps being removed.

Dave and the strange boy she had seen with him were having Cokes, too. Well, she wasn't interested in any of her big brother's friends, either. They always treated her like a not-very-bright kid sister. Next year they would be seniors and would think themselves even more superior.

A husky male voice stopped her.

"Man, am I wiped out!"

Who *was* that stranger? He sounded so much different from Dave's other friends. His rapid, staccato manner of speaking told her he was no Southerner, but that wasn't surprising. Many of the new residents of Holston were from the North and other sections of the country.

The voice itself fascinated her. Smooth and resonant, it was a pleasure to listen to. It was not at all raucous like the sounds Dave's other friends made when they talked.

She paused to listen further. The sound of Cokes being gulped was plainly audible and was followed by loud, manly sighs of satisfaction.

Dave spoke up then. He sounded different, too, when he said, "Nothing like a Coke for that tired, letdown feeling, is there?"

She frowned, puzzled. What was going on in the kitchen, anyway? Why was Dave trying to sound like a bored man-about-town? It was certainly out of character for easy-going Dave.

"Man, this air conditioning feels great," the strange boy went on. "You really need it down here, though. The heat outside is unreal, positively *unreal*. Gets hot in Chicago, too, then a breeze will come in off Lake Michigan that beats any air-conditioning system. Man, what a town. Ever been there?"

"Well, no, er, ah, but I've been to Atlanta and Birmingham and Memphis and New Orleans!" Dave was trying hard to make it appear that traveling was old stuff to him, that he was intimately acquainted with the big cities he mentioned. Teddi almost giggled aloud. Dave had been in the cities he cited, all right, but only for a few hours—long enough for Papa to drive through or stop for lunch. He was obviously trying to make a big impression on the newcomer. But why?

She heard a shuffling of feet and then the newcomer asked in something close to a sneer, "What do you do for kicks in *this* burg, anyhow?"

Dave, to her complete surprise, replied, "Nothing! Absolutely nothing! This is the crummiest, do-nothing town in the whole country, I reckon."

He sounded disgusted beyond belief, not at all like the Dave who breezed enthusiastically from one activity to another.

Teddi could stand it no longer. She *had* to see this remarkable young man who could bring about such a change in her brother. She sauntered into the kitchen. She did not look at the young man, for she had long ago found it wise to appear as aloof with Dave's friends as they were indifferent to her.

Instead she looked straight at Dave and said coolly, "Why, Dave Taylor, how could you say such a thing? There are lots of things to do in Holston."

Dave cocked an eyebrow at her.

"Name one."

"I'll name more than that." Teddi began to count on her fingers. "Bowling, swimming, tennis, movies, and horseback riding on the mountain."

"Mountain?" The stranger's voice echoed from behind her. "*What* mountain?"

Teddi lifted an arm and pointed through the big window over the sink.

"That one," she said firmly. "Old Redwing."

A laugh rang out. "Mountain!" the young man cried. "Do you call that a mountain? Man, you should see the Rockies!"

Teddi, unable to take any more of this mockery, whirled.

Angry words were on her tongue, but she never spoke them. Instead, she had to struggle to keep her composure. The young man was *so* attractive! His voice had conjured up a picture of a handsome, suave, debonair fellow . . . and that was exactly what stood before her. Even with his lips curled in scorn at the ancient upheaval of the earth's crust that they called Redwing Mountain, there was something very, very special about him.

He was very different from Dave's usual gangling, guffawing buddies. Where they were red of face, he was deeply tanned. Instead of standing brushlike in all directions, his short-cut hair was brushed to follow the contour of his well-shaped head.

His Bermuda shorts, long white socks, and white T-shirt might have looked affected on one of Dave's other pals, but they looked just right on *him*. Of all the boys she knew, only Jimmy could compare favorably with this boy.

Then she remembered the conversation she had just had with Jimmy, and she promptly ruled him out. *Nobody* could compare with this young man. No wonder Dave was trying to impress him.

"It's nice around here in the spring," she said lamely. Then a sudden thought struck her and she added brightly, "And where else could you go downtown and see three astronauts all at once, walking right down the main street?"

The young man looked impressed. "You mean that happened here?"

Hands clasped behind her, Teddi nodded vigorously.

"Last week. Friend of mine saw them. And a picture of them was in the paper. One was buying a birthday present for his little boy."

She pressed her advantage.

"The President came here last spring, too, and lots of other important people. . . ."

The boy was beginning to lose interest in the conversation, however. He grinned and peered through the window.

"Hmmm. A mountain," he mused. "I must be looking at it through the wrong end of my telescope." He laughed then, heartily, and Teddi was overwhelmed with his charm.

Suddenly she wanted to make a big impression on him, too. Southern girls, she had heard, were supposed to be soft-spoken and sweet. Well, she would try her best to project these qualities.

With a flutter of her eyelashes, she turned to Dave and asked sweetly, "Who's your friend?"

"Oh, I'm sorry," Dave apologized hurriedly. "This is Rock Baxter, Ted. Visiting the Harrises down the street. His folks are moving down from Chicago later this summer."

Teddi was genuinely wide-eyed over this information. The Harrises! They lived in the big, buff-colored ranch-type house on the Hill. Another Eddie, only much better looking.

Still, it wouldn't be smart to let him think she thought he was anything special. Nonchalantly she took a bottle of Coke from the refrigerator. As Dave handed her a bottle opener, she remarked, coolly, "Welcome to Holston."

Dave then added bluntly, as a sort of afterthought, "This is my sister, Teddi."

Rock Baxter's dark brows shot up.

"Not *the* Teddi Taylor!" he exclaimed.

Suddenly she felt as beautiful and glamorous as a girl on a TV cosmetic commercial. But she tried to keep cool, as though such implied compliments were commonplace in her life.

She tossed her head, in what she hoped was abandon.

"Are there any others?" she asked with a coy smile.

"I hope not," he said, and this time she couldn't really tell whether he was in earnest or mocking her. Then he went on, "You see, I heard of you from my aunt, Mrs. Harris. She has charge, it seems, of recruiting hostesses for some pilgrimage or other. . . ."

"For the festival!" Teddi squealed. Then, hand to mouth, she realized that she was showing entirely too much enthusiasm at the news.

"Yeah, that was it. She read a list of possible candidates for hostesses to my uncle last night and your name was among them. I noticed it was spelled with an *i* on the end and I thought that was real sharp. I like names that are offbeat, not just the same old Judy, Susan, or Linda."

His eyes were warm on her now and Teddi fairly bubbled. "Rock is a nice, different name, too," she said.

"Like it?" He seemed eager now for her approval.

"I think it's just darling."

Teddi poured her Coke into a glass and lifted it to drink. How lucky could a girl be? Here she was—charming a handsome, wealthy boy and, at the same time, learning that she was going to be a hostess at one of the antebellum houses during the Pilgrimage! Tiny Coke bubbles stung her nose deliciously as she drank. Viv and Ruby and Carol and, yes, Jimmy, would stare in disbelief when they saw her flitting gracefully about on the lawn and portico of one of the old homes.

She wished they could see her now, too—Jimmy especially. He would certainly be jealous at the sight of her being so friendly with a handsome scion of such a wealthy family as the Harrises.

So Jimmy wasn't coming to her party! She was no longer disappointed. She would ask Rock to come and then watch the reaction of the guests from Colfax Street!

But what would Rock think of them? Teddi immediately thought better of that idea.

She cast about for something else to say. Turning to Dave, she asked smoothly, "Why aren't you working this afternoon?"

She knew instantly she had said the wrong thing. Such words would shatter the image of a privileged son of wealth that Dave was trying to create.

Dave shrugged. "I was," he replied, "and then I decided I wouldn't." He sent a crooked grin at Rock. "After all, it should be a privilege of the boss's son to take time off if he wants to."

Teddi almost staggered at the impact of that remark. How well she remembered Dave's begging Papa to give him a job on one of his crews. Such a job meant hard work, but it paid well—that was what Dave wanted. He had planned to save as much as possible so that he could buy a secondhand car by the end of the summer.

Papa had been firm on the subject of a car. "Any boy of mine wants a car," he had said, "must earn the money for it himself."

Dave had been jubilant when Papa had given him a job. "But just remember," Papa had warned him sternly, "you are to be treated exactly like the others in the crew."

Dave was flaunting that ruling now! It was a good thing Papa hadn't heard that remark about the boss's son.

"Good boy," Rock said with evident approval and admiration of Dave's independent stand. He set his empty bottle down on the table beside Dave's, and both boys swaggered toward the back door.

Teddi eyed the bottles. More evidence of Dave's effort to appear what he wasn't. Ordinarily he would have put the empty bottles in their carton and wiped the sticky rings off the table. Oh, well, she'd do that for him. She knew exactly how he felt about making a good impression. She had felt the same way, ever since the moment she had first heard Rock's voice out in the hall.

She had made a good impression, too, she was sure of that. Happily she remembered the moment when Rock stopped in the doorway and, looking her up and down, said with an exaggerated drawl, "See you around, Dixie Belle."

A few minutes later she fairly floated out of the kitchen. Giddy over Rock's flattering attitude and the news that she would probably be a hostess during the festival, she still managed to find her room. Before her mirror she stopped and impishly pirouetted. But one glimpse into it and she went limp with horror. Dixie Belle, indeed! She looked awful!

Her dainty yellow dress was a mass of wrinkles from lying on her stomach across her bed. Her hair was awry from running excited fingers through it while following the adventures of Rosalyn Rogers' heroine. On her feet were one black flat and one brown flat.

Rock had been mocking her!

She was aflush with embarrassment when she went down to supper later. As soon as they were seated Papa demanded sternly, "Where were you this afternoon, Dave? When I came back from Mountainside, Newby told me you had taken the truck and driven off and hadn't come back. Why?"

Dave gulped, and a slow reddening crept up his neck to the fringe of his crew-cut hair. Gone was the suavity of the afternoon. Instead, he looked like a small boy caught in the cookie jar.

Teddi felt sorry for her brother—almost as sorry as she felt for herself. Both their efforts to impress Rock seemed to have come to grief.

"Well, er, ah," Dave said lamely, "I came home for a wrench I needed and, well, it was just so hot I decided to stay home for the rest of the afternoon."

He could not have given a worse reply. Everyone around the table saw the muscles in Papa's jaw working. They knew he was making an heroic effort to control his temper.

"Well," he said finally, jabbing his fork into a pat of butter and grimly placing it between the halves of a hot biscuit. "I'm glad the rest of my men don't use the weather as an excuse for knocking off work." He put the biscuit into his mouth and chewed rapidly. "About the second time they did I'd fire 'em!"

"Fire!" Ricky shrieked happily.

Nobody laughed. Dave just gulped again and muttered, "Yes, sir."

No one said another word until Papa, in an effort to clear the air of unpleasantness, spoke up. "I heard today that a brother of Mrs. Harris, who lives down the street, is moving with his family to Holston. Name is Baxter."

Teddi shot Dave a surreptitious look. Rock was his son, of course.

Papa chuckled. "They just might be good prospects for one of my Mountainside houses."

Teddi glanced up, horrified. *Oh, no, Papa,* she thought, *you mustn't insult the Baxters by thinking for a minute they would want one of those dinky little houses in Mountainside! Why, they would be interested only in a luxurious home like the Harrises'.* But she said nothing, just listened to Dave, who, eager to return to Papa's good graces, spoke up. "Their son, Rock, was over here this afternoon."

"Good," Papa grinned. "Best to be acquainted with a prospect before you try to sell 'em something."

Dave, relieved at Papa's levity, went on, "He said that Teddi was on his aunt's list of hostesses for the Pilgrimage in the Blossom Time Festival. Isn't that great?"

You shouldn't have said that, Teddi wanted to cry out. *Rock just made that up! He was only making fun of me when he said it.*

But Papa and Mama were beaming at her, and then at each other.

"Just the sort of thing I hoped would happen to my kids when we moved up here," Papa said happily. He turned to Teddi. "By the way, the pool will be in operation for that party Saturday night."

Party? Teddi looked up, dazed. She had almost forgotten about it.

"You and the kids should have a ball," Papa added with satisfaction.

Dixie looked up, an impish gleam in her blue eyes.

"Teddi won't," she said flatly.

Papa raised a brow. "And why not?"

" 'Cause Jimmy won't be here."

Papa turned to Teddi. "Why isn't Jimmy coming?"

Before Teddi could answer, Dixie piped up, "Boy, did they have a fight on the phone this morning. Wow!" And she rolled her eyes upward and then went into a bit of shadow boxing with her fists to illustrate.

Teddi glared at her.

"Well?" Papa said, waiting for an answer. It was easy to see he was surprised at this turn of events. He was probably thinking of the kiss Jimmy had planted on her cheek that morning just as he had stepped up onto the Robinson porch.

Eyes lowered, Teddi replied in a whisper, "He said he and the trio . . . oh, well, it doesn't matter anyway."

And it didn't really. All she could think of now was some way of erasing the awful image of herself that Rock had taken away with him that afternoon.

But she couldn't tell Papa about that.

10

Slender Threads

"Miss Teddi, way you draggin' yo' feet this mornin' nobody'd spec yo' was havin' a party tonight," Elvira scolded as she put a clean cloth over the bowl of dough she was preparing for a Sunday morning coffee cake. Setting it in a warm place to rise, she turned and watched Teddi giving the top of the counter a desultory swipe with a sponge.

Teddi put a little extra emphasis on a spot in one corner of the tile. "I wish it were over," she said grimly.

Elvira frowned at her.

"Somebody ought to shake you, Miss Teddi—wishin' a party was over before it's even started. And you with a fine new pool all finished and full of water and yo' ol' frien's comin' for a pool warmin'." Her laugh was low and rich. "Pool warmin', that's pretty good, ain't it?"

"Mmmm. I s'pose so."

Elvira arched a brow. "Well, don't you kill yo'self laughin'." Her voice softened. "You moonin' 'cause Jimmy ain't comin'?"

Teddi turned, as irritated with Elvira as she had ever been. "Now, who told you he wasn't? Oh, I get it, Dixie, of course."

"Don't you go gettin' mad at that chile."

94

Teddi squeezed the sponge dry and tossed it into the sink. "Oh, don't worry about that poor little thing. If I got angry at her every time I had a good reason, I'd be angry at her most of the time."

This wasn't true, of course, but she felt so confused this morning. She wished the party were over, and then again she didn't. It should be fun but she was sure it wouldn't be. She hoped Rock would drop by and see how nice she looked this morning, but she hoped he wouldn't come near the place during the party that evening.

Thoughts of Rock, she had to admit, bothered her most this morning. Suppose he did saunter over while the party was going on? Suppose her old friends made as bad an impression on him as she had? Wouldn't he report to his aunt that she was poor material for hostess duties during the festival? There would go her chances for social success on the Hill. Such things hung on slender threads, it seemed.

"Did I hear somebody talking about me?" Dixie stuck her head in the doorway, made a face, and dived out again. She was on her way to the Moores' dressed as usual in her waif-from-the-hills manner.

"Why does she insist on wearing those old rags?" Teddi demanded, turning on Elvira as though she were to blame for it. "First thing you know, folks up here will wonder if she has any decent clothes at all."

As she left the kitchen, Elvira's words followed her. "Now, jest you remember, Miss Teddi, lots of times the things we fret most about never happen at all."

Teddi sniffed as she made her way upstairs. A lot Elvira knew about slender threads and things like that. Mama seemed insensitive to that sort of thing, too.

This morning she had almost flipped at sight of Mama and

Tish chatting over the hedge that separated the Moore yard from their own. From her bedroom window it had been easy to see how bright and beautiful Tish looked in shorts, striped shirt, and barefoot sandals. Mama had looked downright dowdy in comparison. She had worn a new, but, oh, so ordinary house-dress, and a wisp of her hair had loosened from the bun on her head and was flying about.

What were they talking about? she had thought nervously. Was Tish asking about the characters who brought them fresh eggs and vegetables? She had shuddered at Mama's possible reply.

Mama hadn't said anything about the conversation except to remark that Mrs. Moore was very nice. That had been one bright spot in Teddi's morning.

The rest of the day seemed endless. Even watching Ricky paddle about in the wading end of the pool did not cheer her up. She looked her best and Rock didn't even show up to see her. But just wait until she didn't want him around and watch him put in his appearance!

As she had gloomily expected, the evening began all wrong. Fifteen minutes before her guests were due to arrive, Mr. Moore, Tish, Nancy, and Eddie came out and sat down in the patio behind the Moore house. What a view they would have of the arrival of her guests—and the party.

Just as she had feared, a few minutes later Rock appeared around the corner of the house.

"Lost your last friend?" he asked cheerfully as he dropped into a poolside chair beside her. She had known that he and Dave were going bowling. It was just her luck that they hadn't left earlier!

Rousing from her gloom, she tried to match her mood to the moment and the possibilities it held. She knew she looked her best in a brightly printed shift worn over her bathing suit. And her hair, fresh from under the dryer, was casually perfect.

She looked at him as coolly as she could, considering the panic his coming had caused her. "Now what makes you ask that?"

The bowling bag he held slid to the ground. "Your air of utter dejection," he replied. Then he grinned amiably. "Just tell old Uncle Rock all about it," he coaxed. "Perhaps he can help with a bit of well-seasoned advice."

The light in his dark eyes lifted her spirits considerably, for it told her he liked what he saw. This time there was no mockery, she felt sure.

Her own regard for him lifted, also, to dizzying heights. How breezy was his manner! How easily he made pleasant small talk. Jimmy's slow, careful manner of speaking was positively dull in comparison.

She was glad that Jimmy had turned down her invitation to the party. Having broken the ties between them, he had left her free to take advantage of Rock's flattering attention. And Rock was fascinating!

Still, it wouldn't do for Rock to stay with her any longer right now. She didn't want him around when the kids from Colfax Street showed up. She hoped the Moores would look the other way, too, and Mimi. . . .

She cast an anxious eye toward the door that opened onto their patio. Why didn't Dave hurry? Rock, apparently, was not interested in leaving quickly. Casually crossing his feet, he said pointedly, "I'd much rather spend the evening here than bowling with that brother of yours."

Her thoughts spun wildly. Pleasure and dismay mingled within her. *But you can't!* she thought, at the same time wishing he could stay, only under different circumstances. If only she weren't giving this silly pool party!

A car growled up the Hill, and she shrank inside. *Probably the Robinson car,* she thought in dismay. Rock would surely laugh at the ancient automobile, so painfully shined for this momentous occasion.

Lyle had no driver's license, so Mr. Robinson would probably be driving. Undoubtedly he was happy for an excuse to see the Taylors' new house on the Hill. He would be all dressed up, Teddi knew, and would look, as he always did, like a refugee from the Roaring Twenties. Teddi could see him now in his one good suit, blue dress shirt, and wide tie hanging out so everyone could see the palm tree hand painted on it.

Rock's reaction to the sight was something she didn't want to think about!

The car passed the Taylor driveway and chugged farther up the Hill. She relaxed, but only for a second. Another car was coming, and it sounded like a truck.

That would be Mr. Newby in his pickup truck with the tool chest built on the bed. With him would be Carol and Bill, since Bill's family had no car at all. Mr. Newby would be delighted to come. He had been foreman of the crew building the house, so he would be curious to see the finished home. Moreover, he would enjoy sitting around talking to his boss.

It wouldn't be her luck, of course, to have Jack Walker be the first to arrive. His convertible was a neat job and in keeping with other cars on the Hill. Then she would have two attractive boys paying attention to her. . . . The prospect left her gasping. But no, it wouldn't happen, not to her.

The door to the patio swung open and Dave stepped out, bowling bag and shoes in hand. "Ready, Rock?" he called.

"Ready!" Rock replied. He heaved himself out of the chair and, in the same graceful motion, swept up his own gear. He grinned down at Teddi. "Bye, now. Have fun."

Teddi wondered if he was hinting that he knew about the party. How could he know about it? She hadn't told anyone on the Hill. Dixie! She was such a blabbermouth!

She tried to hide the relief she felt at his departure. "I'll try," she said lightly. "You do the same."

With an exaggerated drag to his feet, he replied, "Sure, sure! My favorite pastime is bowling with brothers."

Dave was still trying to impress Rock. She could tell, by the one-finger-on-the-wheel driving he was doing when he brought the Taylor Cadillac out of the garage. Moreover, any other time he would have preferred Mama's little compact car.

She sympathized with his efforts. As a matter of fact, she was happy about them. Dave was the only other member of her family who understood how important such things were if the Taylors were to take their rightful place in life on the Hill.

Now, if only the Moores would go away for the evening. She glanced their way just in time to see them, and Eddie, rise and climb into the Moore car. As it purred away, Teddi felt limp with relief.

Now they wouldn't see her guests arrive, or see them diving into the pool or lounging around it. Viv's bathing suit was really pretty flashy; and so probably would be the suits of Ruby and Carol and the others.

Well, they could come now. The sooner the party started, the sooner it would be over.

At that moment a red convertible nosed into the Taylor driveway. She knew at a glance it was driven by Jack Walker. But who were the boy and girl on the seat with him?

"Hi, there, pal!" Viv cried as she and Lyle stepped out of the car. Teddi stared. Viv looked so different. Then she knew why. Her old friend was smartly outfitted in a new skirt and blouse and her short dark hair had obviously just been cut and set in a beauty shop.

And Lyle—he looked as sharp as Rock in light slacks, sport shirt, and loafers.

They were followed by Ruby and Bill Ashby, from the cramped little rear seat. There was nothing left to be desired in their appearance, either.

"Some layout!" Viv remarked admiringly as her dark eyes darted about the grounds.

"You're so lucky!" Ruby sighed.

"I always did say it pays to have money," Jack said lightly as he came around the front of his little car. His eyes were frankly admiring, too, as he added, "And it couldn't happen to a nicer gal."

Teddi went limp. This was the first time Jack had ever approached her in such a let's-be-good-friends manner. The best he'd ever done before was a nonchalant "Hi" and a nod.

It seemed, though, that Viv and the others should have stepped from Jimmy's car instead of Jack's. That was the way it had always been before.

A sudden tightness in her throat told Teddi she really missed Jimmy. Abruptly she forced him from her mind. Brightly gay, she replied, "It is nice, isn't it, the pool and all! And just wait until you see the *inside* of the house."

"I've been dying to see it for weeks!" Viv squealed. She turned to Teddi. "You'll tell us what fork to use, won't you, chum?"

There was much loud laughter over that remark, and some self-conscious shuffling of feet. Then Terry drove into the driveway, with Carol beside him, and several others she had invited in the back seat. Where had he gotten that car? Teddi knew his folks owned a rather shabby one, and this car was almost brand-new.

Terry followed the others out of it and, in passing, whisked a fleck of dirt from a fender with his handkerchief.

"It's my uncle's," he explained, "borrowed for the occasion with the promise that it would get the best of care."

"He even made us dust off our shoes before we got in," joked Tom Howard, who had brought his steady girl, Liz Cobb, with him. Within minutes, all the other guests appeared, in perfectly respectable cars, also.

Happily Teddi took them on a tour of the house and grounds. With Jack close beside her, solicitously touching her elbow in a gentlemanly way as she went up and down steps, Teddi glowed. So far, at least, her misgivings had been completely unfounded.

Swimsuits were donned in the cabana and soon everyone was splashing and swimming in the pool.

It was a perfect evening for such a party, warm and balmy. Even the moon cooperated, coming up almost theatrically bright over the top of Redwing Mountain, then playing hide-and-seek behind great drifting clouds.

Jack Walker hovered close to Teddi most of the time. "I went to a party down the street last week," he was quick to let her know. "At Tess Graves. Know her?"

"Well, no, not yet, but I probably will soon."

Jack nodded. "Sure, you will. You'll like her, too. She's a slick chick and her old man has money to burn."

Teddi was fully aware of the reason he was so attentive to her. But then, such things were among the advantages of having a successful father, weren't they? She did wish, however, that Papa made his money in a swank office dressed like Mr. Moore instead of running around in a truck dressed in dusty work clothes.

It was still flattering to have as popular a boy as Jack Walker on her list of friends. He would certainly fit in the guest list at her next party, along with Nancy and Eddie and Rock and Mimi Martineaux, and, yes, Tess Graves. It would have to be a separate party to which she invited the Hill crowd. Even at their best, she doubted if the old gang would fit in with them.

The party this evening was going fine, but she wasn't going to press her luck by planning another one like it.

Papa brought out his grill and began heating up the charcoal. That accomplished, he started grilling hamburgers, and the eating began. Everybody sat around the pool contentedly.

Viv sighed noisily. "Too bad Jimmy isn't here," she said. "Now would be the perfect time for him to start a hootenanny."

"Say, it would at that, wouldn't it?" Lyle agreed loudly, and the rest of the old gang nodded.

Teddi jumped up. "How about a substitute?" she said, bringing forth a transistor radio. She tuned it in to a popular disc jockey program.

Viv was stubborn. "A substitute is never as good as the real thing. I still think Jimmy should be here."

"Well, you ask Jimmy why he didn't come!" Teddi said, a wee bit tartly.

"Oh, I *know!*" Viv's dark eyes turned suddenly serious. "But I can't tell. Jimmy'd have a fit if I did. All I can say is you'll all be surprised when you find out what he is doing tonight."

Then she clapped her hand over her mouth as though she already had told more than she should.

"I'll bet," Teddi replied. She shrugged. "Who cares, anyhow?"

Viv opened her mouth to speak, but at the same instant a shriek rent the air, causing all of them to jump. The shriek came from Dixie. It was followed by her cry, "Please come help me, somebody!"

Lyle and Bill and Jack started around the house in the direction from which the pleas had come. Soon they reappeared, helping Dixie drag by the collar a gray, lop-eared dog of tremendous proportions.

Teddi took one horrified look and cried, "That is Mimi Martineaux's Weimaraner."

Dixie faced her stubbornly.

"It's a *dog!*" she said. "And I don't care if it belongs to Santa Claus. It has a thorn in its foot and I'm gonna take it out if someone will help me hold him."

She stroked the big dog's head. Sensing a friend, the creature stopped trembling.

But it took four boys to hold him while Dixie, with a pair of sterilized tweezers, deftly pulled the thorn from the pad of its paw. Then the future vet poured disinfectant generously into the wound and told the boys to let go.

The dog howled with pain and rolled over and over in the grass.

"What are you doing to my dog?" A voice came from the shadows beyond the lights around the pool. Everybody turned to see Mimi Martineaux step into view.

Teddi's heart sank. She might have known that what she had dreaded would happen before the evening was over. Mimi, looking around at her guests, must recognize every one of them and know they didn't live on the Hill. Most of them had been her classmates during the last, brief month at school—and she had done a good job of snubbing them.

Well, there went her chance of ever having Mimi Martineaux come to one of her parties, Teddi thought ruefully.

Dazedly she watched Dixie march over to the Martineaux girl. "He was limping," Dixie explained, "and I saw a thorn in his paw and decided to take it out. And I did a pretty good job if I do say so myself. See, it doesn't hurt him anymore."

She pointed to the big dog who was sitting up now, a sort of bewildered where-did-the-pain-go expression on his face.

Mimi looked down at the small, earnest-faced girl before her and said softly, "I noticed he was limping, too. I planned to take him to the vet tomorrow. But I'm glad you spared him some hours of pain."

Her voice didn't sound one bit snobbish, just sort of wistful. Her face was wistful, too, as she turned and said to Teddi, "I'm sorry I broke into your party." Again her eyes swept the group. "It looks like you were having a wonderful time." Everyone heard her sigh. "Come on, Tex, let's go."

Now Teddi was confused. Mimi sounded as though she wished she had been invited to the party! Come to think of it, Rock could have meant the same thing when he had told her earlier to have fun.

And they would have had fun, too. She was certain of that now.

Elvira had been wrong, she thought, as with throbbing head she tried to sleep that night. It wasn't the things one worried about that didn't happen; it was the things one didn't dream of that did!

Oh, dear!

11

Using the Old Bean!

Things looked different the next morning. Lying half-awake in bed, Teddi was uncomfortably aware of it. Bits of conversation and happenings of the night before came back to her.

The look on Mimi's face that she had thought so wistful now seemed more like scorn. And her words, "It looks like you're having a wonderful time," seemed like sarcasm.

How could she have been so naive as to think the aristocratic Mimi Martineaux would wish she had been invited to a party where the other guests were kids from Colfax Street?

The same thinking applied to Rock, too.

Teddi buried her head in her pillow. Jack's words came floating back, too. "Never let your heart get in the way of your head," he had said. "Gotta use the old bean to get ahead in this world."

Jack was an opportunist, all right; he admitted it. Well, what was wrong with that? From now on, Teddi decided, as she rolled over and punched her pillow with a fist, she was going to be one, too. She was simply not going to let her emotions, or old ties, or any of that sort of thing, divert her from her goal of belonging to the Hill crowd.

This morning Mimi's friendship loomed as a big step on the way to that goal. Somehow she must attain it. That would not be accomplished by wishful thinking, but by following Jack's advice.

That settled, she allowed herself several luxurious stretches. She was glad the pool party was over. Now she was free of any obligations to the old gang. And, moreover, she had shown off her house to them, too.

She yawned. In her new scheme of things Jimmy would play no part at all, she thought with satisfaction. Viv had intimated she would be surprised and delighted when she learned what he had been doing during her party. Like fun, she would!

"Miss Teddi! Breakfast!" Elvira's voice floated up the stairway.

"Coming," Teddi replied, rolling over and covering her head with a sheet.

She was in no hurry. This was Sunday morning when everyone sort of drifted down to the buffet-style breakfast Elvira prepared. There was only one condition: Everyone had to be ready to leave for Sunday School and church by nine o'clock. Mama taught a Sunday School class and Papa went along to keep her company, so it applied to the whole family, except Ricky. Everyone had to tiptoe around so as not to wake him. He often howled when he was left at home.

Teddi lifted the sheet and looked at the small clock on her desk. It was almost eight o'clock! She'd better get started. One bare foot was on the floor when the telephone on her desk tinkled. She yawned again as the foot sought a pink scuff somewhere beside her bed. Someone else could answer it; it was probably for Papa, anyhow.

"Miss Teddi!" Elvira called softly. "Telephone."

"Thanks, Elvira."

Finding the terry cloth slipper, she wriggled her foot into it. Then she found the other and did the same. Shrugging into her robe she walked languidly over to the phone and picked up the receiver, fully expecting to hear Viv start gushing over the party.

She yawned, "Hi," into it.

"Well, hi," came a familiar voice from the other end of the wire. "Did I wake you up?"

Instantly she was on the alert. Jimmy! Well!

"Oh, no, I've been up for hours."

"I'll bet. Say, how did the party go last night?"

"Fine, thanks." Her voice was cool. "Why? Did you think it would fall apart just because you weren't here?"

A tiny thread of shame went through her. Now, that was no way to talk to an old friend like Jimmy. Anyway, it might give him the idea that she had missed him. And she hadn't, not one tiny bit.

But if Jimmy noticed any coolness on her part, he chose to ignore it.

"Well, no," he sort of chuckled, "but I did think it might crack a bit. You still mad at me?"

"Mad? Why should I be mad?" And she wasn't really. Jimmy was an attractive boy, and no girl in her right mind would stay angry at him for long. Still, she shouldn't let him think he could smooth over sidestepping her party as easily as all this. "After all"—her voice stiffened—"I wouldn't want to draw you away from something more important than a little old party at my house!"

Now she was using the old bean! That remark had really put Jimmy on the defensive.

"You know I would have come if I could have," he chided her gently.

"Oh, I do?" she asked archly. "Couldn't you have come? *Really,* now?"

"Well, I suppose I *could* have. But it would have meant passing up something. . . ."

"Ohhh."

"Something that might mean a lot in the future. Aw, this isn't getting us anywhere. What I really called for was to ask you to change your mind about going to that dance at the Rec Hall next Friday night."

Each word of her reply now sounded like a dropping icicle. "I'm afraid not," she said. "You see, I have something else that might be important to my future to do that night. Sorry, I can't tell you what it is."

What a big fib that was. She had nothing special to do that evening, unless staying home could be called that. But there was a limit to the lame excuses a girl should take from a boy for breaking a date.

"Have to go now. Elvira says breakfast is ready."

His answer was hesitant, and definitely disappointed. "Well, so long."

"So long." And she firmly pressed the receiver into place. Then she rose and, without a single regret for her action, dressed and went down to breakfast.

It was plain that the ties with her old friends on Colfax Street were withering. Soon they would break altogether. It was up to her to make real efforts to replace the old friends with new friends here on the Hill.

Her thoughts strayed back to Mimi. With some straight-forward action on her part, she could doubtless become friendly with the granddaughter of Mrs. Pierre Martineaux. Why, last night Mimi had sounded as if she would *like* to be friendly.

During breakfast a delightful thought struck her. She'd call

Mimi and ask if she would go to church with her.

Mimi sounded sleepy over the phone.

"Teddi who?" she mumbled. "Oh, the girl at the party last night. How nice of you to call!"

Teddi glowed. She was making some progress.

"Would you like to go to church with us this morning?" Teddi asked quickly, afraid her courage might fail.

There was a second of complete silence. Then came the hesitant reply, "Ohhh, I don't know. You see, I. . . ."

Teddi thought quickly. "I suppose this is pretty short notice. Another time, perhaps?"

"Yes." The answer was a bit too quick and glib. "Another time."

Teddi forced a gay note. "Okay. Another time. Be seeing you. Bye."

"Bye. Thanks for calling."

Teddi hung up, her pride stung. It had all been so polite—and distant. Then she remembered Jack's words and shrugged. She *had* made some progress. She and Mimi were now on speaking terms.

On the way to church Papa asked Dave, "How did the bowling go last night, son?"

Dave grinned broadly.

"I beat Rock!" he said happily.

"But I thought you expected to be beaten by this city slicker from Chicago," Papa chuckled.

"I did. But I found he talks better than he bowls."

Teddi looked at Dave in complete surprise, although she couldn't blame him for rejoicing because he had bested Rock at something. There was definitely something frustrating about always being the underdog.

During Sunday School she felt Jimmy's eyes on her. He

was trying to get her attention. But she looked straight ahead and stubbornly acted as though she weren't aware of his existence.

Jack gave her a boldly friendly look and walked out beside her from the educational building.

"Aren't you going to church?" she asked as they parted between the two buildings.

"Nope. I just come to please my folks. And one hour a week of this do-good business is all I can stand."

Teddi was shaken a bit, but she supposed it was just part of Jack's rather cynical outlook. She wasn't sure she liked it, however.

After lunch she cast about for something to do. She had just finished reading the last of her Rosalyn Rogers books and decided to go to the library the next day and get another one. But that didn't help now.

She wandered restlessly out onto the patio. A moment later she was startled to see Rock coming toward her.

Sitting beneath the flower-lined umbrella that cast a flattering light on anyone beneath it, she waited expectantly and hopefully. She smoothed the skirt of her beige linen sheath and patted her shining hair. She looked her best and was glad.

Rock's eyes were frankly admiring as he dropped down beside her with a "Hi, honey. How're y'all?"

She had hardly replied with an "I'm fine. And you?" when Dave yelled down from an upstairs window.

"How about going for a horseback ride on the mountain? Sybil says she would like to go."

Sybil? Teddi was surprised that Dave would want to take her along on an outing with Rock. She was Dave's sometimes girl friend from the Colfax neighborhood.

But she didn't dwell on the thought. She was too eager for a date with Rock. Quickly she spoke up. "Oh, we'd love to, wouldn't we, Rock?"

Her gaze turned toward him, and she was shaken for the second time that morning. He looked positively stricken! Or was it trapped?

Didn't anybody want to go anywhere with her? First Mimi and now Rock, hemming and hedging.

Her first reaction was to tell him coolly that nobody was forcing him to go. But somehow she knew that wouldn't be using the old bean. Bold action, that was Jack's way—and hers, too, from now on.

"You do like to ride, don't you?" she coaxed.

Rock sort of gulped.

"Oh, sure I like to ride." He rose and did a bowlegged walk around a circle. "I'm an old cowhand . . . when do we start?"

Dave bounded down the stairs and was soon out on the patio. Hearing Rock's last remark, he said, "Soon as I go pick up Sybil."

"I'll go put on my jeans," Teddi said, mentally resolving to put on her brand-new, faded denim ones.

"I'll get into my riding togs, too," Rock said, eyeing Dave's Levi's and plaid sport shirt. "Be back in a jiff."

Teddi soon returned to the patio wearing her jeans and a polka-dotted shirt with a becoming collar. She was just in time to see Eddie Thomas's white sports car whisk into the Moore driveway.

Why not use the old bean again and ask Nancy and Eddie to go with them? Teddi thought boldly.

Nancy came out to greet Eddie. Seeing Teddi approaching, she waved at her. "Come on over," she said with surprising cordiality.

Then Rock came back and they chatted for a few minutes.

When the coming horseback ride was mentioned, Rock intimated that he was a pretty good rider as there were lots of horse trails in the park along Lake Michigan in Chicago.

Eddie said he liked to ride, too, and so did Nancy. That was the opening Teddi needed to ask casually, "Well, why not go with us? We're going to get horses at the stable on the mountain and take a spin around the trails up there."

"We'd *love* to go!" Tish gushed from behind them.

Nancy whirled. "What about Dad?" she asked quickly.

Tish shrugged. "He's taking a nap. We'll be back before he wakes up and realizes we're gone."

The twins came dashing up.

"May we go?" Tina pleaded.

Tish ground out a cigarette. "Heavens, no," she said impatiently. "You'd just be in the way. I'll go change. Won't be a minute."

She followed Nancy inside, leaving the twins in tears.

"Never mind," Eddie consoled them. "I'll take you for a ride when we get back."

In a few minutes Nancy and Tish returned—in identical outfits. Then Dave drove into the Taylor yard with Sybil Cummins beside him. Teddi liked Sybil. She was a tall, quiet girl and obviously very fond of Dave.

Sybil greeted Nancy and Rock and Eddie shyly.

"Let's get going," Dave said.

Teddi and Rock climbed into the back seat of the Taylor car. Tish, Nancy, and Eddie squeezed into the sports car. Dave drove on ahead and the others followed.

"She's sure lively for an old lady," Rock whispered.

"Who?" Teddi asked, puzzled. He couldn't mean Sybil. She was quiet and looked no older than her sixteen years.

"Nancy's mother," Rock answered.

Teddi was shocked. How could he talk so about the girlish Mrs. Moore? But it seemed Rock was full of mockery this afternoon.

"You call *this* a mountain?" he laughed as the car purred around the curves that led to the top of Old Redwing.

"What would you call it?" Dave asked, his ears reddening.

"A hill, and not a very big one, either," was Rock's easy reply.

They passed a rustic sign that proclaimed they were entering Redwing State Park.

"Man, don't tell me this is a *state park!*" Rock chortled.

Dave's ears got redder with each wisecrack. Teddi began to get a trifle annoyed. Did Rock have to mock everything?

"Yep." Dave replied. A few minutes later, as the car drew up before a shedlike building with stalls in it and corrals all around the outside, he continued, "And this is a *stable,* and those four-legged animals are *horses,* I think."

Rock ignored the biting words.

"Man, cowboys yet!" he crowed as an attendant in cowboy boots, shirt, and big straw hat, led out horses for them. "Alabama cowboys!"

At sight of a certain spotted pony, Dave's eyes gleamed.

"This is the one for you, Rock," he said, handing over its reins.

"Not Paint!" Teddi cried. Somehow she had a feeling that Rock and that pony weren't meant for each other. It looked very gentle, but Teddi knew that if given the reins it could be off like the wind. It was one of Dave's favorites, and Jimmy's, too. But, of course, they could ride like Indians.

Dave gave her an impish look and a wink. "Oh, Roy Rock Rogers won't think he's much of a horse." He turned to Rock. "You can handle him with your hands and feet tied, I'll bet."

"Man, just watch Old Rock!" he snorted, and he swaggered up to Paint and started to mount him. As he put his foot into a stirrup, Paint's flank quivered. The pony shied.

Rock was almost pulled off his feet. "Hold it, will you?" he muttered angrily.

"Take hold of the saddle horn," Dave said as he swung himself easily into the saddle. "Then put your left foot in the left stirrup and swing the other leg over, so."

Rock eyed him coldly. "Thanks, chum. When I need your advice I'll ask for it."

Dave shrugged and grinned while Rock made two more tries before he finally sat awkwardly in the saddle.

Teddi knew then that her suspicions had been well founded. Rock could talk better than he could ride. Those smart remarks had been his way of covering his uneasiness. Rock couldn't admit that he wasn't good at *everything*.

He sat like a broomstick in the saddle. Teddi felt almost sorry for him as they rode out of the corral and down a narrow shady path toward the horse trails.

Dave didn't share her feelings, however. He was taking obvious pleasure in showing off his superior horsemanship to Rock. Once on the trail he and Sybil galloped on ahead. Nancy and Eddie were close behind them.

Teddi was a good rider, too. But now she found herself having to slow her pace to that of both Rock and Tish. And a pretty sad pace that was.

Her ire rose. Dave had a lot of nerve going off and leaving her to cope with Tish and Rock and an unpredictable horse like Paint.

Suddenly around a brushy curve she saw a horse and rider approaching. Teddi would have recognized the rider if he had been a mile away.

Wouldn't Jimmy choose this as a time to go riding? And wouldn't that piece of paper pick the same time to blow across the path in front of Paint?

Resentful at having such a rider as Rock, the pony shied, snorted, and took off. Rock, frantic, loosened the reins instead of tightening them. That was a signal for Paint to pick up speed, which he did immediately.

The trail was narrow and rocky. With two horses coming at each other down the middle, one had to swerve aside.

It was Jimmy, of course, who plunged into the underbrush to avoid a collision. Waiting there for Paint and Rock to pass, he quickly saw that something was wrong. Rock's tense, white face told Jimmy that the horse was a runaway!

Teddi sighed with relief when she saw Jimmy wheel his horse around abruptly. She knew what he intended to do.

He didn't disappoint her. As Paint came abreast of him and his horse Jimmy started to gallop alongside.

By taking the reins of Rock's horse into his own hands, he persuaded Paint to slow down.

Minutes later, Teddi and Tish caught up with them. By that time Jimmy was riding Paint and Rock rode the other horse, a definitely more gentle mount.

She felt grateful to Jimmy, but resentful at the same time. His heroics had certainly put Rock in a bad light.

As Jimmy rode past her, he grinned in his little-boy way and leaned over, asking softly, "That your date for Friday night?"

He was making fun of Rock! Well, she wouldn't stand for that.

"So?"

Jimmy shrugged. Then he slapped the reins against Paint's neck and rode on, whistling softly.

12

The More the Merrier

The sight of the turquoise "squaw dress" hanging in her closet, brought a lump to Teddi's throat. Memories of fun-filled evenings at the Rec Hall came rushing back.

She had often worn the dress while whirling and twirling about the floor with Jimmy, conscious every minute that she looked very attractive. Jimmy had looked just as sharp in cowboy-styled shirts and Levi's. Onlookers had often remarked that they had made a nice-looking young couple.

She felt again the excitement that she had felt while dancing with Jimmy. He was an accomplished square dancer, light and graceful, with an inherent sense of rhythm. When he and the trio had played and sung, as they had often done during inter-missions, it had seemed she could not hold all the pride that had welled up within her.

Before her flashed a picture of Rock riding Paint. How stiff and awkward he had looked in the saddle—and scared, too. The contrast between his horsemanship and the easy manner in which Jimmy rode was painful.

Rock wasn't *always* poised and sophisticated, she knew that now. Nor was Tish always chic and girlish looking. When they had returned to the stable from the ride, Mrs. Moore had been tired and disgruntled, and she showed it.

"No bumpy sports car for me on the way home," Nancy's mother had groaned. "Instead, I want to ride in that heavenly comfortable car of my neighbors."

She had fairly dragged herself into it. From her seat between Rock and Tish, Teddi had cast sly glances at the older woman. With her hair in disarray and skin reddened by the sun, Tish had looked every year of her age!

Could it be, Teddi thought as she caressed the folds of the full skirt, trimmed with yards and yards of silver rick-rack, that she was measuring her family and old friends, as well as her new acquaintances, by the wrong yardstick?

Nothing was all good, just as nothing was all bad, she had heard Grandma say many times. Could there be more truth in that statement than she had realized? She had to admit that the dances she had attended with Jimmy had been more fun than the ride on the mountain with Rock.

A wave of longing for the old times swept over Teddi. If only she could turn back the hands of time!

Suddenly a bright ray of hope appeared.

I could still go to that square dance with Jimmy on Friday night, I'll bet, she thought, putting the dress back between two other square dance frocks.

Why long for something that was easily within her grasp? She frowned thoughtfully. Of course, letting Jimmy think that she had a date with Rock for that evening did complicate matters. Why had she done that? How high the price one paid sometimes for a moment of satisfaction.

Use the old bean, Jack had said. This was the time to do just that. Surely there was some way of getting the message through to Jimmy that she still wanted to go to that dance.

I could call him up, she thought forthrightly, *and tell him I didn't mean it when I said if he didn't come to my party I wouldn't go to the dance . . . and that I was just teasing when I made him think I had a date with Rock.*

But no, she wouldn't do that! Jimmy *hadn't* come to her party and hadn't given a good excuse for not coming! She felt miffed again.

But when she looked at the dress again, back came the memories of all the fun she had had at those dances. Yes, and with her parents along, too. The Taylors, the Robinsons, the Newbys, and the Bryants had been members of the Rocking Rockets, a group that met every Friday night at the Rec Hall, to wheel and deal to the tune of old-time music.

Even Grandma and Grandpa Taylor had gone once in awhile, as each member was free to bring guests. Nobody at the Rec Hall called the old folks characters. She could remember how proud she had felt of her grandparents as they danced sprightly around the floor.

Wasn't there some way of letting Jimmy know how she felt without calling him up and . . . well, her pride wouldn't stretch that far!

A sudden inspiration came to her. She would call Viv and casually say she was looking forward to the dance Friday night. Viv would immediately dash to the store and tell Jimmy what she said, Teddi knew. Viv undoubtedly knew of the latest developments in their relationship. Viv and Jimmy were just like brother and sister, confiding their troubles to each other. Viv would be happy to patch up any rift between Teddi and Jimmy, just as Jimmy would do the same for Viv and Lyle.

Her mind ran on. After Viv had delivered her message, Jimmy would think he had misunderstood Teddi. He would certainly call to set the matter straight. If he questioned her, she could laugh it off as a big joke. The same could hold true of her "date" with Rock. Jimmy would be glad to see things her way, she was sure he would.

She hastened to the telephone on her desk. Halfway through dialing the Robinson number, her finger stopped. What excuse could she give for calling Viv? After all, she mustn't be too obvious about her intentions.

Dixie solved this problem. Sticking her freckled face through the doorway of Teddi's room, she asked, "Wanta see a swell picture this afternoon? *Lobo* is on at the Lyric."

Lobo, Teddi knew from the advertisements running in the *Holston Times,* was a new production which told the story of a noble dog accused of killing some of the sheep he had been set to guard. In the end it was proved the sheep had really been killed by the wolves he had just chased away.

It was the kind of story Dixie loved. Come to think of it, Viv liked stories like that, too.

"I'd love to!" she replied to her small sister's query—with so much enthusiasm that Dixie looked surprised. Then she added, as a sort of afterthought, "I think I'll ask Viv to go along, too."

"Okay," Dixie replied, skipping away. "The more the merrier."

Teddi went back to the phone. This time she finished dialing the Robinson number.

Viv answered the phone and listened while Teddi hastily presented her plans. Her voice was cool when she replied, "No, I can't go. And even if I said I could, how could I be sure you'd be there to meet me?"

Teddi blinked. It wasn't like Viv to talk like that.

"You mean you don't think I keep my word?" she asked

cautiously, trying to conceal the fear in her voice.

"Only if it happens to suit your fancy."

"Now, what do you mean by that?"

"Well, take the example of the dance Friday night. You told Jimmy you would go and then, because he couldn't come to your party, you told him you wouldn't. All because you had made a date with that Chicago cowboy you were out with yesterday!"

Teddi preened. Imagine a rumor going around that two boys were crazy about her! No girl would deny that.

"Who told you about him?"

As if she didn't know! Only one person could have given Viv *that* information.

"Oh, the old grapevine," Viv replied vaguely. "Grows pretty thick around here, you know."

"Especially between the Robinson house and the Bryant store?"

Some of Rock's wit must be rubbing off on me, Teddi thought with satisfaction. After all, Rock *was* witty.

Viv giggled. She couldn't stay angry long, especially at Teddi.

"Well, Jimmy did come over and weep on my shoulder," she admitted. Her tone turned scolding. "You shouldn't treat him like that. Why, you are turning him into a real woman hater!"

Teddi replied heatedly, "Well, just remember he *didn't* come to my party and he never gave a good reason for staying away."

"He had a good reason."

Teddi could feel her anger rising. But she remained cool enough to reason that she wouldn't get anywhere pursuing this tack. Use the old bean, she told herself. So she turned suddenly sweet and purred, "Oh, I'm sure he did. That's why I'm so anxious to go to that dance Friday night. I thought maybe he might tell me why he didn't come."

Viv gasped. "You mean you *are* going? But Jimmy said. . . ."

"Jimmy was looking for sympathy; remember?"

"How 'bout that? Say, when does that show start?"

"In about an hour."

"Meetcha in front of the Lyric then. Bye."

"Bye."

Jubilantly Teddi replaced the receiver. Her plan had worked so far. She could see Viv now, sprinting over to Bryant's grocery store. Viv would bring a message from Jimmy with her to the show, a message that he was pleased she had decided to go to the dance. Then he would call her tonight.

Ricky toddled in then and she picked him up and set him on the bed. Then she took the small, bright book he had brought with him and read him the story of *Chicken Little*. He listened happily, repeating some of the words after her. Then, taking the book from her, he slid off the bed and toddled out again in search of someone else to read it to him.

As he left Dixie came in again. She was dressed, as usual, in shabby jeans with shirttail out. Teddi decided not to reprimand her. Perhaps she was too critical of her small sister. She hadn't really dressed up herself. They were just going to a show with Viv, weren't they? She didn't have to impress Viv. It was nice sometimes *not* to feel she had to impress somebody.

If Rock or Nancy or Mimi were around, she would dress up. After all, it was important that she look her best when they were near, especially Rock. His aunt had not yet asked her to be a hostess at the Pilgrimage. She still had to make sure he took back good reports of her.

But she wouldn't see Rock this afternoon. He had gone to a nearby town with his aunt to visit relatives.

"Ready?" Dixie asked.

"Ready," she replied. Following her bouncy sister down the stairs, she announced with pleasure, "Viv's going with us."

Dixie did two hops on one step and one hop on the next, her straight hair flying up and down like a mop being shaken. "So is somebody else," she said.

"Not one of your little friends from Colfax Street, I hope." Teddi stopped, anxiously envisioning the two girls running up and down the aisle for popcorn, pop, and candy bars.

"Friend of mine, but she's not so little and she's not from Colfax Street." She took a last hop on the bottom step. "She's waitin' outside for us."

With a flourish Dixie opened the front door and pointed. There, sitting on one of the white wrought-iron chairs on the portico, was Mimi Martineaux!

"Why didn't you ask her to come in?" Teddi cried, horrified. What must Mimi think of her family.

Dixie shrugged. "I did. But she said she'd liefer wait out here. Didn't you, Meem?"

Teddi was so confused she didn't see Mimi's nod. All she could think of was Dixie's using an old country expression like *liefer!* Couldn't she realize that such things put them in a class inferior to the Martineauxs? And that outfit of Dixie's. It looked simply awful beside Mimi's crisp dress.

And why didn't I change? Teddi wailed to herself.

It was too late now. All she could do was to try to make a good impression through conversation.

"Well, hi, there," she said in a low, restrained voice. Her laugh was restrained, too, when she added, "I hope this picture is as good as Dixie thinks it will be."

Mimi gave her a long look. It was neither friendly nor unfriendly.

"A picture about dogs is bound to be good," she said flatly.

Teddi was taken aback. Here was someone who liked animals as much as Dixie, and she'd better be careful what she said.

Mimi turned to Dixie. "You didn't say someone else was going with us," she said, as though she had been betrayed.

Teddi swallowed a rising anger. Why didn't Mimi want her along? Did she think she was better than Dixie's big sister? But that was silly reasoning. Mimi was going to the show with Dixie, wasn't she?

Her desire to have Mimi for a friend returned full force. Here was her first real chance to become acquainted with the elusive Miss Martineaux, and she was determined to take advantage of it. So she ignored the remark and its implications.

Mimi rose abruptly. "We'd better get going if we don't want to miss the first of the show. I hate to get in after it has started. Spoils the story, I think, don't you?"

She was speaking to Dixie.

"I certainly do," Dixie agreed, and they were on their way.

She might as well not have been along, Teddi thought, for all the attention they paid to her. Gab, gab! She had never seen Mimi as talkative as she was now with Dixie.

When they reached the narrow, brick sidewalk Teddi had to drop behind. But Dixie and Mimi didn't even seem to miss her.

They talked mostly about animals. Mimi gave a full report of Rex's healing paw and then told of a family of squirrels making their home in an old oak tree on the Martineaux grounds.

Dixie told Mimi all about Cottonblossom and why the goat had been sent to the farm. Mimi was properly sympathetic about the loss of Dixie's pet.

This pleased Dixie and, encouraged by Mimi's attitude, she enthused, "You must go to Grandpa's farm with us the next time we go. I'll show you Cottonblossom and all the other animals out there!"

"I'd love to go," Mimi replied warmly.

Teddi panicked at the idea. She'd have to throw an obstacle in the path of those plans. What was Dixie thinking about, anyway, inviting Mimi out to that old farm? Why, they were likely to find Grandma outside working in her garden with a sunbonnet on her head!

She felt miffed, too. Why would Mimi accept an invitation from Dixie and yet not go to church with her older sister?

They turned into Calhoun Street and headed toward the downtown section of Holston, some ten or twelve blocks away. In passing through this old section of the city, they seemed to be stepping back a hundred years in time. The lovely old houses must look much as they had then. This part of town was very different from the bustling city growing up around it. The girls walked slowly, savoring the taste of a slower-paced, more gracious past.

Emerging from the shade of the old trees that overhung the brick walk and the street, they were abruptly popped back into the present. An overhead traffic light turned red, stopping an olive green, soldier-chauffeured limousine with two high-ranking army officers sitting stiffly in the rear seat. In crossing the street in front of the car, Teddi noticed the trim, smiling, young Japanese men walking ahead. They were obviously trainees of the Army Missile School at the Arsenal. And the two German-speaking ladies just behind them were probably wives of German scientists making their homes in Holston.

Holston was truly a cosmopolitan city, Teddi thought proudly, and a far cry from the sleepy little southern town it had been before the moon boom.

They passed in front of the ornate county courthouse, soon

to be razed and replaced by a towering structure of shining chrome and glass. Right now people were hurrying up and down the worn marble steps like scurrying ants.

Teddi shook her mind free of such thoughts and tried to dwell on how nice it would be to see Viv. Viv! The thought of Viv startled her. What would Mimi think of noisy Viv? Noisy? Loud was a better word.

It just wouldn't do for those two to get together, she determined suddenly. But how could it be avoided?

Approaching the theater, she caught a glimpse of Viv, frantically waving to her from the front of a line of boys and girls waiting to get in. An idea came to her. Mimi and Dixie were so engrossed in each other they would never notice.

When they stopped at the end of the line, she saw her chance. Slipping away from them, she moved to where Viv was standing. Handing her ticket money to Viv she said, "Get my ticket, too."

Viv grinned at her. "That's why I came early, so I could be at the head of the line and get our tickets first."

Teddi smiled back. Good old Viv, even if she wasn't in the same league as Mimi Martineaux. She stepped into the outer lobby and bought two sacks of popcorn, two candy bars, and a bag of roasted peanuts.

"Gee, thanks," Viv smiled gratefully when she saw the purchases. "This should keep us from starving."

They went into the darkened theater well ahead of Dixie and Mimi Martineaux.

13

Plans Astray

"I told Jimmy he had misunderstood you," Viv informed Teddi as soon as they sat down. "I told him you wanted to go to the dance with him Friday evening. But"—she stopped long enough to take a bite of candy and chew it thoroughly—"he said he had understood you perfectly. He asked me to tell you he had an engagement for that evening, anyhow. He said you would have to make it another time."

Even in the darkened theater Teddi could see the inquisitive look in her friend's dark eyes. *What has happened between you two?* it seemed to ask. Teddi fought a rising tide of resentment that Jimmy should have put her into this position.

"You tell him for me," she whispered, "that there just might not be another time."

She meant it, too. Her encounter with Mimi, and the walk to the show with her and Dixie, had sent her thoughts flowing in an entirely different direction. Her biggest desire now was to become friendly with the Martineaux girl. Somehow the dance had slipped to a place of secondary importance.

With effort she had a good chance of making it a reality. First she'd have to get rid of Viv, and she would do that as soon after the show as she could. Then she would rejoin Mimi and Dixie. There must be some way she could join their cozy little circle.

The story unfolding on the screen was just a blur of dog, sheep, and Alpine scenery.

She didn't care if Jimmy hadn't fallen for her little scheme. But what was the other engagement he had for that evening? She was curious in spite of herself. It just wasn't like Jimmy to act this way.

Did he have a date with another girl? An attractive boy like Jimmy could have all kinds of dates if he wanted them. She sent a suspicious look at Viv. Was her old friend twisting the situation to suit herself? She had always liked Jimmy. But Teddi knew that Viv had a date with Lyle for that evening.

Had a date with this mysterious girl been the reason he hadn't come to her party? Her thoughts skimmed over a long list of possible girls. She couldn't think of a single one that Jimmy could ask for a date without her knowing about it.

Wait a minute! Two weeks ago Jimmy's trio had performed for a money-raising function at Buckhorn High School. There were lots of pretty girls at Buckhorn. Jimmy had probably met one and fallen for her and was now dating her.

Wasn't he the sly one? Her spirits ebbed. Then she straightened up determinedly. What did Jimmy Bryant mean to her, anyway? Nothing. Absolutely nothing.

She would be glad when the show was over and they had squeezed their way out of the theater. She'd see to it that Viv took the first bus going her way. Then she would find Mimi and Dixie and walk home with them. She would make an all-out effort to join in their conversation, during the course of which she would invite Mimi to her house for a swim.

She could see Jimmy now, a look of sadness on his face.

He'd feel badly because she was no longer his special girl friend. His eyes would sorrowfully follow her and Mimi making their way through the halls this fall at school. He'd look even more sorrowful when he saw how chummy she was with Rock and Jack and Tess, and perhaps Nancy, who had said yesterday that she might go to the public school this fall.

"You'll change," Jimmy had said. And she had, for a very good reason. A girl from Buckhorn was the cause of it!

Just as they stepped from the circle of light cast by the flashing theater sign, Viv's bus went by.

Viv shrugged. "Oh, well, I don't have to hurry home, anyway." And, taking Teddi by the arm, she practically dragged her into the drugstore that adjoined the theater. "Let's get something to eat. I'm starved."

They hurried toward the one empty booth and reached it just in time to find that someone else had reached it ahead of them.

"Be our guests," Dixie beamed up at them, pointing to the empty spaces beside her and Mimi Martineaux. Viv accepted the invitation with enthusiasm.

"Thanks, pal, old buddy," she crowed, plumping down beside Mimi. Awed and subdued when she had met Mimi at the Taylors', Viv was her breezy self at the drugstore.

"Oh, you're no stranger!" she cried when Mimi was introduced to her. "I saw you at school last spring even if you didn't see me. And I saw you when you popped up at Teddi's pool party. You live in that big old house on the Hill, don't cha? With your grandma?" Viv rolled her dark eyes and clucked her tongue. "It must get pretty dull up there with her. I know I wouldn't want to live with mine, no siree! She's nice and I love her, but boy, is she old timey!" She turned to Teddi, who was sitting, acutely embarrassed, across the table from her.

"You know, don't you, Ted, how green my grandma gets when she sees a girl in shorts or holding hands with a boy?" She shook her short-cropped dark head.

"My parents are strict enough, but my grandma's a lot worse." She swung back to Mimi. "Where are your folks, anyhow? In California someplace, aren't they? Oh, sorry, chum." She looked up at the patient boy waiting to take her order. "Make mine a strawberry malt. And put a little strawberry in it, will you?" She laughed heartily at her own wit.

She had been right, Teddi thought miserably, when she had thought that Viv simply didn't fit into the scheme of things when Mimi was around. Mimi, it was plain to see, was shrinking under Viv's verbal barrage. In fact she had blanked out, conversationally, and in all other ways.

Hands folded in her lap, Mimi stared straight ahead as she ordered a cherry Coke. Her lips were tightly compressed all the time she waited for it.

But that had no effect on Viv; she simply turned her attention to Dixie and chattered on.

Teddi regarded Viv in an increasingly critical light. Common, that was what she was. The difference between her and quiet, withdrawn Mimi was appalling.

"Boy, is she queer!" Viv exclaimed later as she and Teddi parted outside the drugstore. "I'm glad she doesn't live close to *me!*"

Whereupon she broke into a run for the corner where a bus going her way was grinding to a stop.

Teddi was limp with relief. She turned and hurried to join her sister and Mimi.

"You and Dixie were right." Teddi tried to join in their conversation. "*Lobo* was a great picture."

Mimi regarded her stonily. "It was, wasn't it?" she replied

stiffly. That was all she said to Teddi on the walk home, though she talked freely with Dixie.

Viv certainly fixed things for me as far as Mimi is concerned, Teddi thought bleakly as she made ready for bed that evening.

She punched her pillow and rolled over. She'd simply have to keep her old friends apart from the new. It was the only way she could make the impressions she desired. Sleep was a long time coming. Restlessly her mind went over and over the same ground. She must especially try to keep Rock's good opinion of her. Upon it might rest her chances of being a hostess at the festival.

If she were a hostess, perhaps that would help erase the bad opinion Mimi must have of her now.

The possibility of floating around the lawn of the Martineaux mansion in a hoopskirted dress sent her off into a pleasantly hazy dream. Her face, beneath the wide, droopy-brimmed hat tied with a satin bow under her chin, was sweet and lovely. The image was further enhanced by the basket she carried which was rapidly being filled with great yellow roses she was snipping from the bushes that grew about the portico of the stately old house on the Hill.

It would be the Martineaux mansion to which she would be assigned as hostess, she was sure of that. The dream reached a climax with her and Mimi walking arm in arm down a white, shell-packed path bordered with boxwood.

She was still thinking about it the next morning—and laying plans to help bring it about—when Dixie burst into the house and raced up the stairs.

"Hey, Teddi!" she cried, bouncing into her room. "Wanta hear a good joke?"

Mama came out of Ricky's room across the hallway, her finger to her lips.

"Shhhh," she cautioned. "You'll wake the baby."

Dixie lowered her voice. Her giggle almost choking her, she went on, "Mrs. Moore, you know, Tish, well, she just asked me if I would tell those old folks from the country who deliver our vegetables to stop at her house and she would buy some from them, too!"

Teddi's knees turned to the consistency of soft soap. The possible consequences of this little "joke" left her limp. Had Tish told Dixie what she had said about her grandparents? Would Dixie tell Mama? And would Mama tell Papa? Oh, dear!

"And what did you tell her?" Mama asked quietly, entering the room.

"I told her those old folks from the country were my grandma and grandpa and they didn't bring eggs and vegetables to anybody but us."

"Good girl," Mama said approvingly, patting Dixie on the head.

In spite of her worries, Teddi felt admiration for her little sister. Why hadn't she been as honest?

"What did she say then?"

Dixie shrugged.

"Nothing. She just looked sort of funny and said she was sorry."

Teddi went limp with relief. Tish and Nancy might avoid her now that they knew about her grandparents, but at the moment that did not seem important.

Then Dixie added, "Mrs. Harris was sitting on the Moore patio and heard the whole thing. She got a big laugh out of it."

Teddi didn't laugh at that bit of news. There went her chance of being asked to serve as a hostess during the festival, she thought sadly.

Papa didn't laugh, either, when Dixie repeated the story during lunch. The muscle in his jaw quivered as he asked grimly, "Now, how did Mrs. Tish ever get an idea like that in the first place?"

Teddi gulped. She felt grateful to Tish for keeping her secret when Dixie replied, "I dunno."

After lunch every member of the family went his separate way. Teddi headed for the enclosed part of the patio where she settled herself on the chaise longue. Clasping her hands behind her head, she brooded over the way her plans had gone wrong.

The doorbell startled her.

"You get it, Miss Teddi," Elvira called from the kitchen. "I'm bakin' and my hands are all floury."

Teddi rose slowly. It seemed to her that Elvira should take care of such duties as answering the doorbell. She sighed, feeling quite sorry for herself, and started down the hallway toward the front door.

She was shocked when she opened the door, for there, standing on the portico, was Rock's aunt, Mrs. Harris!

"Why, hello, Mrs. Harris," she stammered. "Do come in!"

Mrs. Harris smiled warmly as she stepped inside. "I was just returning from our Women's Club meeting," she said, pulling off her white gloves, "and thought I would stop by and chat with our new neighbors for a few minutes."

Teddi's spirits zoomed. Mrs. Harris had stopped by to ask her to be a hostess at the festival, she was certain of it. She had just presented her list of candidates for the posts and Teddi Taylor had been approved by all the club members.

Finally one of her plans was working out as she had intended!

"We're so glad to have you," she beamed.

From the basement came Mama's muffled query, "Who is it,

dear?" Teddi shuddered. Mama had chosen the worst possible time to throw those shag rugs into the automatic washer. The word would spread quickly on the Hill that Mrs. Tate Taylor did her own laundry! That would end any chance the family might have of standing on an equal footing, socially, with the other residents.

If only she could quietly slip away, Teddi thought despairingly. Instead, she struggled to keep her composure.

"It's Mrs. Harris, Mama, Rock's aunt," she answered, at the same time ushering their guest into the living room.

There her composure went to pieces. What a mess that room was! Papa had been reading the paper and, as was his custom, had left the pieces scattered all over the floor.

"Do sit down," she said, flustered. Hastily she began gathering up and folding the offending pages of the *Birmingham Register*.

A Coke bottle, half hidden beneath one piece, was dislodged by her efforts and rolled across the floor. She retrieved it, wondering bitterly why Papa always had to drink a bottle of Coke while reading the paper.

Then she noticed that Elvira hadn't dusted that morning. What must Mrs. Harris be thinking of the Taylors?

"Mama will be here in a minute," she murmured.

Mrs. Harris smiled at her again and settled herself comfortably on the sofa. Crossing her legs at the ankles, she said, "I should have called before but I have been so busy with the festival."

I was right, Teddi thought excitedly. *She did stop to ask me to be a hostess.*

Then Mama came bustling in and her hopes faded. Never had Mama looked so dowdy! Her face was flushed from her exertions, and wisps of hair were flying everywhere. She was dressed in a faded, worn housedress and had an apron tied about her waist.

But Mama made no apologies for her appearance. She came swiftly forward and greeted Mrs. Harris while, at the same time, she wiped her damp hands on her apron.

With Coke bottles and papers grasped firmly in her arms, Teddi fled to the kitchen.

14

Big Bad World

Elvira took the kettle off the burner of the electric range and poured the boiling water over the leaves in Mama's most delicate china teapot.

"I'll fix the tray, Miss Teddi," she said firmly. "You carry it in and serve."

Teddi looked at her and said tentatively, "It would look better if you did it."

Elvira arched a brow at her. "Why?" she asked, placing cups and saucers on the tray beside the cream pitcher and sugar bowl.

"Because if you do Mrs. Harris will think we have a maid," Teddi replied.

Elvira eyed her disapprovingly while, with skillful fingers, she arranged on a small plate the crisp cookies she had just taken from the oven.

"That would be pretendin' somethin' that ain't," she said wryly. "I'm the cook and part-time cleanin' woman. Sometimes I do the ironin'. But I don't know a thing about servin' tea and ain't aimin' to learn."

With that she turned and went about her other work.

Teddi gazed at the plump back, her eyes tracing the bold pattern in the crisp cotton dress. She sighed. If Elvira refused to do something there was no use arguing with her.

Teddi picked up a cookie from the cookie sheet. She bit into it and chewed slowly, her taste buds fairly purring.

"Luscious," she murmured to the stubborn back.

Elvira turned and gave her a warm, appreciative smile. "I likes to cook and bake," she said simply. "I do best what I likes to do."

Teddi picked up the tray. If she had to play maid, she had to, that was all. But she'd bet that Mrs. Harris would think it queer to see a young lady of the house perform so menial a task. *She* probably had several maids about her big house, as well as a butler or two.

Resolutely she walked down the hallway toward the living room. She could hear the low murmur of voices followed by a light laugh. That was Mrs. Harris, she knew. Mama's laugh was low—almost harsh, Teddi thought sometimes.

What was Mrs. Harris laughing about? Probably something gauche that Mama had said or done.

Teddi straightened determinedly. She would show Mrs. Harris that there was one in her family who had all the social graces.

The step down into the living room, which Papa had been so proud of when he built the house, was her undoing. She was so intent on making the grand entrance that she forgot all about it.

The remark Mrs. Harris made just as she stepped into the room didn't help any, either.

"My nephew, Rock?" Mrs. Harris's voice sounded puzzled. "But I have no nephew named Rock."

Down Teddi went, her shriek resounding around the big

room. Stumbling, she lurched forward. Cups, saucers, spoons, and cookies cascaded out in front of her.

It felt like a fall from a high cliff, and just as scary. For a second she was completely dazed. Then the sight of the heavy pot of hot tea sliding toward the edge of the tray brought her back to her senses. With amazing presence of mind and dexterity, she righted the tray and pot, though she remained off balance herself.

"Oooooh." Mrs. Harris waved a nervous hand in front of her face. "That was close."

My last chance to be asked to be a hostess is gone now, Teddi thought miserably. *Mrs. Harris must think me much too awkward for so demanding a role.*

"Dear, are you hurt?" Her mother's anxious query came through her blurred consciousness.

"No, I don't think so," was Teddi's uncertain reply. She was hurt all right, but not physically.

With difficulty she straightened up. Holding the tray steady so the teapot would not slide off, she made her way to the coffee table where she set it down. Then she went about helping Mrs. Harris and Mama pick up the debris.

When everything was straightened out again, and fresh cookies and cups and saucers and spoons brought from the kitchen, Teddi was invited to sit down and have refreshments with them.

While Mama poured, Mrs. Harris turned to her and smiled. To Teddi's surprise it was a warm smile, with more than a faint suggestion of Rock in it.

But Mrs. Harris had just said she had no nephew named Rock!

"There is something I want to ask you," Mrs. Harris said to her while accepting a cup of tea from Mama.

Hope spurted up in Teddi. Could it be, after all that had happened, she would be asked to serve as hostess, anyway?

Teddi waited breathlessly.

Mrs. Harris bit into a cookie. Surprised delight registered on her face. Wrinkling her nose, she bit again. Then she turned to Mama and asked, "These cookies are positively marvelous. Did you bake them?"

Mama shook her head. "No, I'm afraid not," she smiled. "My cook, Elvira, did."

"Mmmmm," Mrs. Harris murmured as she took another bite. "I wish I had a cook who could bake like this." She shook her head wistfully. "As a matter of fact, I wish I had a cook. I can hardly boil water myself without burning it."

Teddi looked at their visitor in surprise. That was an oft-used remark of Grandma Taylor's, though not about her own cooking, which was superb. But where had the elegant Mrs. Harris heard such a common, old saying?

Mama nodded understandingly. "Good cooks are hard to find," she said sympathetically. "Good household help in general is. I know I am fortunate to have Elvira. She has been with us for nineteen years." She lowered her voice. "Though goodness knows, we do have to humor her something frightful to keep her happy here."

Mrs. Harris sighed. "I humored my last cook frightfully, but she left me anyway. She said she was going to New York to visit a sister. I haven't been able to replace her, and my poor husband is getting dyspepsia from eating my cooking. And I am completely worn out from doing all the cleaning and cooking."

She took another cookie while Teddi stared at her in amazement. Mrs. Harris did all her own work! Even her cooking! The thought of this elegantly clad woman pushing a sweeper, or shelling peas, or rinsing dishes for the dishwasher was simply staggering.

"Since my nephew Robert has come to stay with us until his parents move down from Chicago, it has been much worse," the woman went on. "You know how boys are, leaving everything lying around. I do so wish I could find an Elvira. I would cherish her like the jewel she is, believe me."

To Teddi's disappointment, whatever it was that Mrs. Harris had intended asking her was put aside while she and Mama launched into a discussion of the difficulties of finding and keeping household help these days.

Wonder and amazement filled Teddi while she listened. Mrs. Harris did not have several maids or butlers . . . she had no help at all . . . her nephew Robert was staying with her until his parents moved down from Chicago.

Mrs. Harris and Rock looked so much alike. Yet Mrs. Harris had no nephew named Rock. Were Rock and Robert the same boy? Teddi had to clear that up.

"Did you say your nephew's name was Robert?" she asked innocently, when the opportunity presented itself.

"Yes, Robert Baxter. He's my brother's son," was the reply.

Teddi's mind did a fast spin while Mrs. Harris turned to Mama and said, "My name was Baxter before I married."

So Rock *was* Robert! That was the only way it could be. A suspicion edged into the corner of Teddi's mind while she saw Mama frown thoughtfully, then smile.

"When I was a little girl in Worley," Mama said, "we had neighbors named Baxter."

Mrs. Harris's brows rose. "I lived in Worley," she said.

Mama gasped and, pointing a finger at her guest, cried, "You? On College Street?"

Mrs. Harris nodded vigorously. "I was Eileen Baxter."

Mama's voice rose. "I would never have guessed. Well, I was Nellie Martin."

Mrs. Harris squealed. "Why, your mother was my second grade teacher. I was crazy about her. Is she still living?"

"Very much so. Right here in Holston."

"Well, I never. It's a small world, isn't it? I must go see her. You see, I was gone from this part of the state for years and lost touch with people."

Mama nodded. "That is so easy to do."

Teddi sat stunned. Mrs. Harris and her mother had once been neighbors and friends, of sorts. Again the picture of her hoopskirted dress and floppy brimmed hat appeared before her. Would the mental picture have a better chance of becoming reality now?

She managed to ask, "Mrs. Harris, is Rock your nephew's nickname?"

Mrs. Harris frowned thoughtfully.

"Rock? Rock? Well, I never. . . . Is that what he calls himself?" A look of amusement spread over her face. "Well, it does sound impressive, doesn't it?"

She dismissed the matter with a laugh.

Teddi didn't laugh. She felt a sort of bond with Rock. They had both done the same thing, really; they had both given themselves names they thought more in keeping with the new images they were trying to build. *Teddi. Rock.* The names Thelma and Robert were commonplace beside them.

"My brother and his wife Alice will be here next week," Mrs. Harris continued, nibbling on her third cookie. "He is being transferred here. I am so glad." She sipped her tea. "They, too, will live with us until they can find a house. Alice says she wants to buy."

Teddi saw the gleam in Mama's eye and moaned inwardly.

"My husband has some nice houses to sell in Mountainside Estates," Mrs. Taylor suggested.

Teddi fairly curled up inside. Why didn't Mama leave well enough alone? Although Mrs. Harris had turned out to be an old friend and neighbor, this didn't mean that Mama should try to sell her brother one of those dinky houses in Mountainside.

"They are in the middle-priced group, aren't they?" Mrs. Harris, surprisingly enough, seemed interested.

Mama nodded.

"Well, Alice wrote that was what they could afford. So I will certainly tell them about those homes when they arrive."

Teddi's disapproval of Mama's tactics melted a little. Mama had often said it was a wife's duty to help her husband all she could, and Mama certainly tried.

Mrs. Harris turned again to Teddi. Now, it was coming, Teddi exulted; now she would be asked to be a hostess.

"Hey, everybody, look what I've got!" Dixie's exuberant voice turned everyone's head toward the doorway. "Isn't he darling?"

And she indicated a big, battered-looking, ginger-colored cat that she held tightly in her arms.

"Where did you get that?" Mama asked in alarm.

"I didn't just get it," Dixie grinned back. "I've been feeding him for a week. But today was the first time he would let me pick him up. He's a stray, I guess. I've been all over the neighborhood trying to find his owner, but I couldn't."

Teddi gave her small sister a look of disgust. Only Dixie would go to the fine homes on the Hill to ask if anyone owned this sorry-looking old cat!

Suddenly the cat gave a yowl and broke loose from Dixie's grasp. It streaked across the living room and skimmed over the coffee table, narrowly missing the teapot and cookies. Another spring took it over the back of a sofa and past a startled Mrs. Harris. From there it sank its claws into the satin draperies and made its way up to the valance. From that vantage point the cat glared down at them.

Dixie watched its progress anxiously.

"We've got to get him down," she said, "before he falls and hurts himself."

"Hurts himself?" Mama moaned, covering her eyes with her hands. "What about my draperies?"

Unconcerned about such things as draperies, Dixie climbed upon a chair and reached for the cat. Her efforts were rewarded by the swipe of a paw of her feline friend.

"Help me somebody!" she cried indignantly.

"What's going on here, anyhow?" Papa's voice boomed from the doorway. Beside him was Mr. Moore, dressed in a pair of rumpled pants, an old shirt, and battered hat that made Papa's crisp work clothes look positively fashionable. He grinned amiably at the ladies and then at the cat.

"Better get a stepladder," he said. Both he and Papa started back the way they had come.

"I see Art's been working in his yard," Mrs. Harris commented. "He was telling me the other day he can't find a satisfactory yardman."

Within seconds Papa was back, without Mr. Moore. He soon retrieved the cat.

What will happen next, Teddi thought despairingly, *to keep her from asking me to be a hostess?*

Papa grinned at Dixie. "You'd better get a cage for this one, honey," he said, scratching the top of the animal's head. "He's a *wild* cat."

Mama was fingering her silken draperies. Several pulled

threads and tiny rips marked the cat's progress to the top. She shrugged and said, "When there are children about the house, such things will happen."

Honestly, thought Teddi disgustedly, Mama and Papa spoil Dixie something fierce—and then let their older daughter practically shift for herself.

Just as she feared, their guest hastily looked at her wristwatch and picked up her purse and gloves.

"I must go," she said. "It is past time to put a roast in for dinner." She hesitated just before reaching the door, and again Teddi's hopes rose. But Mrs. Harris only laughed and added, "My husband has had sandwiches two evenings in a row. I don't dare fix them again."

But even in her haste she stopped to chuck Ricky under the chin. The youngest Taylor had just toddled in from the kitchen where Elvira had been keeping an eye on him. *Everybody got attention but me,* thought Teddi as their guest took her final leave.

As Mrs. Harris stepped off the portico Dixie streaked out the door and shouted, "Hear of anybody needs a good mouser, let me know!"

A faint "I will" drifted back.

Teddi was disconsolate. Mrs. Harris had said it was a small world. But to Teddi it seemed a big, bad, discouraging one.

15

Forgetfulness Runs in the Family

All eyes were on the television set and the hilarious antics of the addlepated father of the series, "The Old Homestead."

Mr. Taylor took a handful of popcorn from the big bowl set in the center of the low, round table before him. Popping it into his mouth, a kernel at a time, he laughed heartily, along with Mama, Dave, Dixie, Teddi, and Rock.

Rock had strolled over after dinner that evening. There wasn't a thing to do around the Harris house, he had said in a bored tone of voice. And, as long as he had to spend a dull evening, anyway, he thought he might as well spend it with others.

The Taylors had laughed at his deadpan manner of speaking. They knew it was his way of saying he had come to see Teddi.

Teddi had welcomed him warmly. He was beginning to seem like one of the family—not nearly so different from them as he had at first seemed. His calling himself Rock had been his way of impressing *them*. So they were really very much the same.

It was a good feeling, Teddi decided, to be at ease with Rock.

She was tired of trying to dazzle him.

It was pretty dull around the Taylor house, too, that evening. So everyone had gathered in the recreation room to watch the "tube," which was what Rock called it.

"What a nitwit he is!" Papa exclaimed at a particularly spineless action of the head of the series family. He grinned at Ricky, sound asleep in Mama's arms. "I see the picture has already put one of us to sleep!" Then the commercial came on and he turned to Mama and said, "I almost forgot. While I was in the old neighborhood this afternoon the Robinsons and Bryants asked us to join them at the Friday night square dance at the Rec Hall."

Mama looked up, her dark eyes shining. "You said we would?" she asked anxiously.

"Of course I did," Papa replied with enthusiasm. "I think it will be great to have one of those neighborhood affairs like we used to have."

"So do I," Mama agreed contentedly.

"Well, I don't!" Teddi said decisively.

All eyes turned her way. Dixie's twinkled mischievously. "No wonder," she snickered. "You and Jimmy are still on the outs."

Papa's brows shot up. "Teddi, do you mean you and Jimmy haven't made up that little spat yet?" He turned to Rock. "Well, why not take this young man instead? He'll go, I'm sure."

Teddi was horrified. After all, she and Rock weren't *that* chummy. Not chummy enough, anyway, for Papa to force him to go to a dance with her.

Why couldn't Papa tend to his construction business and leave her date life alone? Papa never believed in beating around the bush about anything; he always used the direct approach to solve any problems that he might encounter.

Still, Dave had done almost the same thing Sunday when he had asked Rock if he would like to go riding on the mountain. She hadn't minded then. Were her present feelings now caused by the fact that she really didn't want to go to that dance? She didn't want to see Jimmy with a girl from Buckhorn?

A girl from Buckhorn. What better reason could she have *for* going? Especially with Rock. Wouldn't that show Jimmy how little she cared whom he dated?

But, could Rock square dance? Or would he look as painfully out of place on the dance floor as he had on horseback?

She shuddered at the thought of Jimmy's grinning smugly as she and Rock flopped about the floor while he and his date skimmed about the dance floor.

Rock's voice brought her back to unhappy reality. "Sure, I'll go. Might be good for some fun. I'm an old square dancer from away back."

He threw back his shoulders in an exaggerated gesture of supreme self-confidence.

There he goes again, Teddi thought, talking the way he had talked before he mounted Paint. Does he have to pretend to be an expert at *everything*?

She heard the smack of Papa's fist hitting the palm of the other hand. "Say, how about putting a square dance record on the player?" he cried. "Then clear the floor and set up a square? My dancing could stand some brushing up."

"Mine, too," said Mama, and she left with Ricky to put him to bed.

Everybody rose and scurried. Soon the turntable of the record player was stacked with several square dance numbers in which the music and calling were combined. Then the furniture was pushed out of the way.

"C'mon, squirt," Dave said to Dixie, pulling her to the center of the floor.

Papa took Mama as a partner and Rock took Teddi.

"It takes eight dancers to make a square," Rock said as they faced each other. "I know *that* much about square dancing."

And that is probably all he does know about it, Teddi thought miserably. How awkward he would look compared to Jimmy!

"I know that much about it, too," Papa grinned, "but I thought we could practice a bit with six." Then, looking through the sliding glass doors to the patio, he added, "What about them?"

Outside stood Nancy and Eddie ready to rap on the glass. Dave sprinted to the door. "Come in and join us," he said.

"I love to square dance!" cried Nancy.

"That makes two of us," said Eddie as they scooted in and took their places.

The music started. The caller on the record sang out: "Bow to your partner, then bow to the lady in the corner."

To Teddi's surprise Nancy, Eddie, and Rock seemed to know exactly what to do. The lively strains of "Melindy Lou" continued and the caller cried:

> "Men to the center,
> Do si do,
> All the way 'round
> Rock to and fro."

About the room they whirled and twirled. There was much laughing when someone failed to perform the maneuver called. Teddi was ashamed of her critical thoughts about Rock, for he followed the calls quickly and easily. It was she who failed to make a proper turn!

"That square dance class in junior high is coming in handy now," Rock grinned at her. "I hated it at the time. Goes to show one never knows, does one?"

"One certainly doesn't!" Teddi replied happily.

> "Ladies to the center and the gents sashay,
>   Circle to the left in the same old way,
>   Take your girl to the side of town,
>   Circle up four and don't fall down. . . ."

On and on the music went, and the calling and dancing, too. Teddi was exuberant. Rock was a wonderful square dancer!

"You were marvelous," she said after several sets.

"Was I?" he asked, a serious look suddenly coming over his usually carefree-looking features. "Then perhaps it makes up for my poor showing on that horse Sunday."

Teddi felt shaken. Wasn't Rock as sure of himself as he sometimes sounded? He must, at some time, have had feelings of inadequacy. Why else should he call himself Rock? How well she knew that only someone who wanted to improve his image would have done such a thing.

She and Rock sat down breathlessly beside Nancy and Eddie.

"Gee, that was fun," Nancy laughed, stretching her legs out in front of her. "Wasn't it, Eddie?"

Eddie nodded. Then when his breath had returned, he said, "And strenuous, too."

Dave looked their way. "Why don't you two come to the square dance at the Rec Hall with us Friday evening? We always have a ball at those affairs." He shook his head sadly. "Guess I'll have to settle for the squirt here as a partner. Sybil has left town for a few days with her grandparents."

Nancy smiled happily. "We'd love to go," she said. "Wouldn't we, Eddie?"

"We certainly would," Eddie replied emphatically.

Nancy let her feet fall to the floor with a little thud. "And Tish and Daddy are playing bridge that evening with the Atkins," she continued smugly. "Isn't that a break? We can go without them, Eddie."

Eddie gave a self-conscious chuckle. "Speak for yourself, Nan. Don't get me tangled up in that mother-daughter feud."

Nancy spoke up quickly. "But it isn't a feud, really," she protested. "It's just that my mother has to keep proving to everybody that she is still a teen-ager at heart." She rolled her eyes and sighed heavily. "Everywhere I go she has to go; everything I do she has to do."

"Mama is going to the dance," Teddi reminded her.

Nancy shrugged. "But your mother will act her age," she said quietly. "She won't get out on the floor and do a solo of the Charleston or some other Stone Age dance and embarrass you to pieces."

The picture of Mama doing a solo on the floor before a lot of people sent Teddi off into a gale of laughter. No, Mama would never embarrass her like *that*. In other ways, perhaps, but not. . . . Her laughter stopped abruptly. Nancy's mother sometimes embarrassed *her,* even as her own did! Teddi reeled at the revelation.

Mama appeared with a tray of Cokes. "Have fun, kids," she smiled as she set the tray down. She quickly retreated.

"See what I mean?" said Nancy. "If that had been Tish, she would have sat down with us and in no time made herself the center of attention."

"Nancy," Eddie reproved, "you shouldn't talk about your mother like that. She has lots of *good* qualities."

Nancy took a sip of Coke and grinned impishly.

"I know that," she shrugged. "But I guess I want to be the

only teen-ager around the house."

They talked a bit longer and then a dip in the pool was suggested.

"Plenty of suits in the cabana," Papa offered, having overheard the remark when he came back for his pipe. "Take your pick."

Teddi could see that Papa was pleased. The pool was turning into a teen-trap after all. Papa and Mama were really pretty sharp sometimes, she concluded.

No one noticed Dixie disappear around the corner of the house. When they emerged from the cabana, they saw her waiting by the pool—with Mimi Martineaux beside her!

"I asked Meem if she'd care to come down for a dip," the freckled one explained simply. "And her grandma said it sounded like a good idea."

Mimi cast her gaze speculatively about the group. "I hope I'm not barging in," she said softly. To Teddi's surprise, she sounded as though she really hoped she wasn't.

"Not a bit!" Dave cried. Coming forward, he grinned at her. "You know Nancy and Eddie, don't you?"

"Not so well as I should like to," came the soft reply.

Has she changed, or have I? Teddi thought in bewilderment. She seems so much more outgoing than she had the afternoon they had gone to see *Lobo*. Suddenly she knew the reason for Mimi's changed attitude; the Martineaux girl was now among her own kind. There was no loud-mouthed Viv to make her withdraw into herself. She thought about this while they dived and swam and splashed.

She noticed that, despite the friendliness of the others, Mimi stayed close to Dixie. "Mimi acts like she is all set to run if she has to," Nancy said in a low tone as she and Teddi climbed out of the pool together.

Teddi nodded absently. She was busy thinking. Should she act on an impulse she had had a moment before? She must use the old bean, she reminded herself. When Mimi came near she asked boldly, "Would you like to go to the square dance with us tomorrow night?"

Even before she had finished asking her question, another thought made her half regret her action. Viv and the old gang would be at that dance. And she had learned, hadn't she, that they and Mimi simply did not mix?

She was torn between two desires. She wanted to keep Mimi away from her old friends, and she wanted to show her off to them, too!

She could picture their entrance into the Rec Hall the next evening. It would be a sensation!

"The Taylors are really flying high," she could hear the onlookers whispering. "Look who they're running around with. And Teddi! The boy with her is the nephew of Mrs. Harris who lives on the Hill. He's from Chicago. And the tall, solemn-looking girl with them is Mrs. Pierre Martineaux's granddaughter! The blonde is Nancy Moore! And Eddie Thomas! Wow!"

Dave had overheard her question. "Say, I wish you would go, Mimi," he said earnestly. "With me."

"What about squirt?" laughed Eddie.

"She can find herself a partner nearer her size."

Mimi seemed pleased, and flustered, too.

"Yes, I will go," she replied after a brief hesitation. "I'm sure Grandmother won't object. She said this morning that I should get out more with young people. In fact"—she came very close to laughter—"she almost pushed me down here when Dixie came up and asked me to come."

Mimi was more relaxed from then on, and she seemed to

join in their conversations more easily. She did, that is, until Nancy remarked again that she was glad Tish wasn't coming to the dance.

She turned to Mimi and smiled, "You don't have my problem, do you?"

"Problem?" Mimi's brows furrowed in puzzlement.

"Oh, your mother always butting into everything you do."

A shadow passed over Mimi's face. The old look of sadness returned.

"No, I don't have that problem," she said wistfully. "In fact, neither of my parents seems to care what I do, much less want to do it with me."

Teddi could see Mimi beginning to withdraw again.

"Why don't folks stop talking about her mama and papa?" Dixie whispered fiercely. "It always makes her sad."

Now Teddi knew why Mimi was partial to Dixie's company. Dixie was simply more perceptive than the rest of them.

She hoped that Mimi wouldn't change her mind about the dance. Apparently she didn't for when Dave rose to walk home with her, she made no objection.

"Well, I guess I'm no longer needed," Dixie flipped as she watched her brother and Mimi go down the drive. Quickly she turned and skipped into the house.

Teddi watched her, a new appreciation of her little sister growing within her.

Rock lingered for a few moments after the others had gone. They sat silently, until he turned to her with a suddenness that made her jump. "Do you know what?" he exploded. "I almost forgot what I came over here for this evening."

Teddi flapped her lashes at him, at the same time asking coyly, "Wasn't it to see me?"

Rock laughed. "Well, sure, of course. But also, just as I

went out the door Aunt Eileen told me to ask you if you would be a hostess at one of the old houses during festival week? I guess she meant to ask you this afternoon while she was here, and, well, I guess forgetfulness runs in our family."

Teddi was overcome with delight. Still she managed a calm, "Well, don't forget to tell your aunt I'll be glad to."

16

Surprise Secret

The eyes of every dancer were on the Taylor party as it strolled into the Rec Hall the next evening. Whether sitting on the chairs that hugged the gray walls, or on the tiered benches on one side, or lounging around the soft drink stand, they turned as one and stared at the newcomers. Or so it seemed to Teddi.

She had expected it, of course, yet the glow of the spotlight almost made her blink, anyway. Pride coursed through her, too—pride and pleasure in being an important member of such a distinguished group.

Flying high, that was what the Taylors were doing. And didn't they deserve to? Papa was now a very important man about Holston. And their guests. . . .

She could hear the whispers going around.

"Isn't that Mimi Martineaux with Dave Taylor?" the dancers asked with the same awe they would have shown had she been a European princess.

"And that handsome boy with Teddi? Isn't he the nephew of Mrs. Harris?"

"It didn't take long for her to forget Jimmy Bryant, did it?

And that stunning blond girl with the group. I know she is Nancy Moore, whose father is the attorney. And the boy with her is Eddie Thomas, the architect's son."

So it went, though Teddi did see some dancers who weren't paying any attention to them. But they were some of the new people in Holston, she was sure, and couldn't be expected to know the importance of the occasion.

She wished Papa wouldn't greet everybody in the same way that he had in the old days. And Mama was just as bad— asking everyone about their families. One would think the Taylors still lived on Colfax Street!

That didn't prevent her, however, from walking, chin up with pride, beside Rock. She knew he looked sharp. Where was Jimmy? She hoped Jimmy saw Rock now; he wouldn't smirk as he had done on the mountain. She could hardly wait for them to start dancing. That would really startle Jimmy. He would certainly regret not coming to her party!

Not for anything would she let Jimmy know she was giving him even a tiny thought. But, she did cast cautious glances around, hoping to see his sad and wistful face.

She was surprised to see the casual way in which Dave was acting. Imagine, escorting Mimi Martineaux with the same nonchalance he would have shown toward Sybil Cummins! Nothing seemed to impress him anymore since he had found the crack in Rock's self-assured armor.

There was Jimmy! She recognized him, though all she could see was his back. The nerve of him. He had missed their grand entrance entirely!

Her anger flared and then dimmed as quickly. He was only pretending he didn't know she was here, she could see that. The deep discussion he was having with two boys—the rest of the trio—was only a cover-up for his true feelings.

Viv waved at her from a spot not far from where the boys were standing. Teddi waved back half-heartedly. She mustn't encourage Viv. First thing she'd know Viv would be over, overwhelming Mimi and Nancy with her exuberance.

Why didn't Jimmy turn around so she could ignore him?

The trio was obviously more important to him than she was. Of course, they were fine entertainers and their popularity had been snowballing lately.

Still, that was no excuse for him to ignore her presence. Or was it a girl from Buckhorn that was causing his indifference?

Where was she? Teddi looked around, but she could see no girls, except Viv and Ruby and Carol, anywhere near the entertainers' stand.

Rock, unaware of her wandering thoughts, looked about the room and returned to his old ways. "You call this a Rec Hall?" he asked with cynical amusement. "Man, I'll bet the acoustics in this old barn are just jim-jim-dandy."

"Oh, they're just super," Teddi replied, tearing her attention away from the tableaux across the floor.

Dave turned and grinned at Rock. "Well, you said you were coming for kicks, didn't you? The sound effects will be one of them. But I'll guarantee you that when the dancing starts you won't even notice."

Someone suddenly jolted Teddi's elbow.

"Well, who do you think you are? A queen or something? Trying to get by with practically ignoring an old friend?" Viv's giggle sounded beside her.

Startled and dismayed, Teddi turned and stammered, "What made you think that? Hi, there, Vivian."

Why hadn't Viv waited until she was ready to speak to her? She would have, too, when she could have slipped away without her guests' noticing. She thought of Viv's encounter with

Mimi in the drugstore and hoped Viv would act with a little more reserve this time. But Viv was as unrestrained as ever.

"Oh, you don't need to be so formal!" she cried. "Vivian! How do you like that?" She turned toward the rest of the Taylor group. "Who are your friends?" She pointed to Mimi and said, "You I have met."

Teddi became so flustered that Dixie had to take over and introduce Nancy, Eddie, and Rock to Viv. Then Carol and Ruby came over and she repeated the introduction. Lyle and Terry and Bill remained near the stand where Jimmy and the trio were still talking.

Soon Viv and Carol and Ruby were talking with the Taylor guests. Carol and Ruby were a little shy; Viv, however, was at her brash best, it seemed to Teddi.

Teddi was thoroughly embarrassed when Viv suddenly grabbed her arm and dragged her in the direction of the platform. "There's an old friend of yours over here who wants a word with you," she explained.

When they stopped Teddi found herself facing Jimmy. He was as surprised and embarrassed as she was.

Viv! She was as bad as Papa at butting into her date life. She wasn't ready to greet Jimmy, she hadn't made up her mind how she was going to treat the girl he had brought with him.

Should she play it with coolness, indifference, or jealousy? She had no time to decide, however, for Jimmy, recovering from his surprise, smiled at her and said smoothly, "Long time, no see."

"Yes, it has been, hasn't it?"

He looked away for a second as though trying to think of something else to say. Then he nodded in Rock's direction. "I didn't think you'd be here tonight," he said. "Not with *him*."

Teddi gave a toss of her head. "I didn't expect to be here,

either," she replied, trying to be casual. "Then Papa said we had been especially invited and insisted that Rock and I come with the family."

There was an awkward pause while both groped for another subject. They'd never had this trouble in the old days, Teddi thought unhappily.

Teddi forced a bright smile. "Are you and the boys going to play and sing tonight?"

Jimmy shrugged. "In a way, yes; partly, anyhow."

He was avoiding a direct reply again, just as he had done when he had said he couldn't come to her party. It was so exasperating.

"What do you mean by that?" she demanded, words coming more easily now. "Either your trio will play and sing, or it won't. Isn't that right?"

Jimmy ran his fingers through his short hair, ruffling it into an appealing little-boy look.

"Well," he said. "Not exactly. I mean, part of the time we'll sing and part of it, well, that's my secret." A mysterious smile played about his lips. "You'll see soon enough. Then you'll know what I was doing the night of your party."

Of all the evasive answers, this one was the best! It was plain to see he was giving her the runaround. "Oh, you!" she sniffed. But should she care what Jimmy was going to do? She was with Rock and. . . .

"My hero!" Rock's voice came from beside her. She turned to see him grinning at Jimmy. "Man, you're some horseback rider. In that department I'll have to admit you're a better man than I am, Gunga Din."

Jimmy eyed the tips of his loafers. "I wouldn't say that," he replied modestly. "Anyone that can hang onto that Paint when he's off and running is doing mighty well."

"That was a kindly remark if ever I heard one. Thank you, kind sir."

Rock bowed slightly and they laughed. The tension was broken. Viv and Lyle joined them then, and they chatted for a few minutes. Everything was friendly; almost too friendly, Teddi thought. It did seem that Jimmy and Rock could show a little jealousy.

Suddenly over the mike came Art Blake's call. "Choose your nearest partner and square up!"

Rock took Teddi's hand and led her to the square being formed by the Taylor party. Lyle led Viv to another square, made up of Colfax Street neighbors. Jimmy, she noticed, didn't choose anybody. He just resumed his talk with the other members of his trio.

The music started and the dance got into full swing. Square dancing was not a new experience for Mimi, she soon realized. The Martineaux girl followed the calls expertly.

"You're a peachy square dancer!" Teddi laughed admiringly into Mimi's ear as they whirled past each other.

"Oh, square dancing is all the rage in California!" Mimi replied gaily. She certainly seemed to be enjoying herself this evening. Was it partly due to the fact that no one had yet asked her about her parents? It must be pretty depressing to have parents who weren't interested in you, Teddi thought.

She hoped Jimmy noticed that Rock was a good dancer. But whenever she looked in his direction, his back was turned. He and the rest of the trio certainly had a lot to talk about.

That silly trio! It seemed so important to him. A girl would be less competition, she thought. Girl? She hadn't seen any girl around Jimmy.

The members of their square changed with the next dance. Mama and Papa joined the Colfax Street neighbors. Viv and

Lyle joined the one in which Teddi and Rock danced. Viv's bouncy dancing and clowning soon had them all laughing heartily. Somehow, Viv's antics didn't seem out of place in the Rec Hall, Teddi decided.

When the music ended and the dancers moved off the floor, Rock said, "Man, I'm thirsty!" Before starting for the soft drink stand, he asked, "Coke, anybody?"

"One for me!" Viv cried. Then, after the other girls had signified their choice, she added, "I'll get it myself." She swept off with Rock.

"She's a character, isn't she?" Nancy laughed. There was no malice in the remark, Teddi noted. Had it been the same when Tish had called her grandparents characters?

At that moment Art Blake spoke through the mike. "Ladies and gents, we will now have an intermission. Get your refreshments, settle down, and make yourselves comfortable. You're in for a surprise and a treat."

The treat, Teddi knew, was the appearance of the Jimmy Bryant trio. But what was the surprise?

"I know what it is," Viv laughed, when she noticed the puzzled look on her friend's face. "I've kept it a secret so far, so I guess I can do it for a few more minutes."

It was the same secret Jimmy had spoken of, Teddi knew, but what was it? The suspense was dreadful.

The crowd was soon seated and waiting expectantly.

With a wave of his hand at Jimmy and the other two boys, Art went on. "All of you know Jimmy Bryant's trio, as most of Holston has seen and heard them at one time or another."

A wave of applause swept around the room—warm, friendly applause. The boys were popular and well liked.

Teddi and Viv sat side by side on the lower tier of seats, with Lyle and Rock beside them. There was an expectant glow in Viv's dark eyes as she leaned forward, chin in her cupped hands. Lyle, too, had a pleased expression.

Teddi's curiosity was suddenly overwhelming. This secret surprise must be something pretty special to cause such emotions in her friends.

The rest of the Taylor party was assembled about them.

"These boys are *really* good," Teddi heard Nancy say. "Aren't they, Eddie?"

"They certainly are," was the earnest reply. "I've heard them several times."

"As you know, these boys are mighty fine performers." What was Art building up to? "And it seems such things get around." He paused for a second, as though gathering his forces. "Just a few weeks ago a talent scout for Regal Records heard them sing. Right on the spot he asked them to record the song—with another of their specialties on the flip side!"

A gasp of amazement went around the hall, followed immediately by more applause. "Yaaaa!" yelled Viv, clapping wildly.

Teddi sat dazed. In a happy blur, she saw Jimmy and his partners shuffling their feet and staring at their loafers self-consciously. In spite of his talent with a song and a guitar, publicity like this was painful to Jimmy, she knew that. It was this very shyness that was a great part of his charm.

Jimmy was such a nice boy! She was happy for him. She leaned forward eagerly to hear the rest of Art's announcement.

"A recording session was set up for a week ago last Saturday evening," Art went on. "And the disc was made."

A week ago last Saturday evening! Teddi was stung by the words. The evening of her pool party. This was the reason Jimmy had not come.

She knew why he hadn't told her about it. He had never been one to brag. Besides, he had often said that the things which look like they would turn out big are the ones most apt to flop! Best not to talk about them until they are over and the results are in. The news had probably come to Viv in one of his unguarded moments, and then he had sworn her to secrecy. That was the way Jimmy operated.

"Tonight we're going to play that record," Art went on proudly. "This will be its first public airing since it was released this afternoon." He picked up a record, looked down at it as though a little dazed himself, and added softly, "It's called 'Redwing Mountain.'"

Very carefully Art slipped it onto the turntable and set the needle down on it. Everyone waited in breathless silence.

Like one in a trance, Teddi heard Jimmy's guitar and voice sound sweet and clear in the lead part.

"Oh, I was born on Redwing Mountain
Seems a million years ago. . . ."

Oh, no, it could not be! Their song! She and Jimmy had written it together one afternoon in the backyard of the Taylor home on Colfax Street. This was, she knew, part of the secret surprise he had mentioned.

It all came back to her now. After listening to the latest top song on the local hit parade, the sad ballad of another mountain in another state, they had laughed and said, "I'll bet we could write a song, too."

They had chosen Redwing Mountain as a subject and were off. Jimmy wrote a line and she wrote the next. Within an hour they had several verses completed. Before Jimmy had left that afternoon, he had picked out a simple melody for it on his guitar. They had both been pleased with the results.

But she had never expected this to happen!

Surprise secret? Secret surprise? It was both—and more!

17

Certain Girl

When the song ended and the applause that followed died away, Art Blake took the record from the turntable and flipped it over. Then he faced the audience and chuckled. "Jimmy tells me he wants to dedicate 'Redwing Mountain' to a certain girl of his acquaintance." He set the record spinning and put down the needle. "He says she will know who he means. It seems she helped him write the lyrics."

Why that's me! Teddi thought, startled.

Everyone else in the hall knew it was she, too, for Art Blake looked right at her while he made the announcement. Immediately she felt their eyes upon her. Some of the glances were amused, some curious, and some frankly envious—especially those of other girls her age.

To be singled out as the certain girl of such a celebrity didn't happen every day. There wasn't a girl in the hall who would not have been proud of the distinction.

Teddi felt proud, too. She sat up very straight. She hoped she projected a feeling of humility as well as pride. She felt humble. She had been so completely wrong about Jimmy. Dear, loyal Jimmy.

Nancy leaned over and said in unabashed admiration, "You?" Then, with a shake of her blond head, she added, "Gee whiz."

Rock leaned over and remarked, "A celebrity yet!" He looked pleased to be sharing the spotlight with her.

Another opportunist, she thought, *just like Jack.*

Eyes sparkling, Viv turned and crowed happily, "Didn't I tell you?"

The rest of the family party, including Mimi, leaned toward her and clapped their hands silently. Teddi looked down at her hands in embarrassment.

She didn't feel embarrassed; she felt like a queen. Dear Jimmy, she thought, sharing his good fortune with her. She was his certain girl. She would always be his certain girl. But what about Rock? He was just a boy with whom she had come to the dance.

Her stay in the spotlight was brief, however. Attention left her abruptly and swung back to Jimmy's trio.

The flip side of the record was played, followed by another round of applause. Then the boys stepped onto the platform and played and sang the two songs just as they had recorded them. The applause was deafening.

Teddi clapped right along with the rest of the audience, at the same time smiling at the envious-looking girls standing near her. Her thoughts whirled. Jimmy Bryant, a big recording star! Teddi Taylor, his certain girl. Teddi was overwhelmed!

The boys played and sang several other songs. Two were audience-participation numbers. The intermission wound up in a rollicking hootenanny.

When the trio finally stepped down off the platform Nancy grabbed Teddi by the arm. "Say, how about introducing us to your singing friend, Certain Girl?" she suggested mischievously.

"After all, you surely can't expect to keep a charming fellow like that all to yourself."

"I should say she can't," Mimi spoke up pertly.

Dixie pushed her way among them. "Wanta join my Jimmy Bryant fan club?" she demanded, her face glowing with excitement.

Nancy looked down at her. "I didn't know there was such a club."

"That's because I just started it. I've already made myself president."

"Put me down as a member," laughed Nancy.

"Me, too," said Mimi.

"Okay," Dixie wet a pencil tip with her tongue and wrote down their names. Then Viv joined, and also Carol and Ruby. Before she had a chance to ask Teddi to join, Nancy repeated, "Well, what about that introduction?"

Teddi tossed her head. She felt confident.

"Come with me, ladies," she smiled. Arm in arm, she and Nancy and Mimi approached the platform.

Jimmy and the boys were surrounded by admirers asking for their autographs. But Teddi knew that when he saw a certain girl coming he would stop, break the circle, and make way for her and her friends.

Jimmy looked up and saw her, all right. But he made no effort to move. Instead, he went right on signing autographs!

She stopped suddenly. Jimmy's lack of encouragement changed her plan. She wasn't going to force her way to *him*. If she did, he would probably think she was being friendly simply because of his new status.

All this attention had probably given him a swelled head, anyhow. The looks of adoration on the faces of some of the girls around him were positively revolting. Letting him know

that Mimi Martineaux and Nancy Moore were eager to meet
him would only heighten his good opinion of himself.

I won't do it, she thought. *I simply won't.*

"Say, what's wrong?" Nancy joked. "Afraid we'll take him
away from you?"

Teddi tossed her head. "Of course not!" She forced a gay
smile. "But how could we get through that crowd around
him?"

"Hmmmm," Mimi murmured. She looked as if she regretted her boldness. "I think you're right. Later, perhaps."

Nancy nodded in agreement, at the same time shaking a
finger at Teddi. "Don't you forget."

Teddi gave a little laugh of relief. "I won't."

Thank goodness, she was out of that difficult situation.

Art Blake stepped out on the platform again and dropped
another bombshell.

"Tune in on 'Tune Time' tomorrow morning, folks!" he
cried. " 'Redwing Mountain' will hit the airwaves then. After
that, watch these boys. They're on their way."

As she and Nancy and Mimi returned to the family group,
Teddi gave a backward glance at Jimmy. What effect was that
announcement, and its implication of more admiration, having
on him? None that she could see, for he was still busily signing
autographs.

The rest of the evening was a blur to Teddi. She was in the
spotlight, and she wasn't. She tried, in what she thought was a
casual manner, to catch Jimmy's attention. But every time she
looked his way, he seemed busy acknowledging the admiration
of a fan.

Certain girl! Ha! A lot that meant.

She missed call after call, tangling the square in which she
danced. At first Dave and the others laughed at her mistakes

and quickly covered for her. But after awhile, they became disgusted.

"Listen, Certain Girl," Dave admonished. "Come down out of the clouds."

"Sick or something? Lovesick, maybe?" There was something deeper than teasing in Rock's voice. "You came to the dance with me, remember?"

That snapped her out of her hazy mood for awhile. This was no way to treat Rock. After all, his aunt had asked her to be a hostess during the festival.

Festival! The prospect brightened her outlook. Perhaps Jimmy was the center of attention this evening. But just wait. . . . Again the picture of hoopskirts, droopy-brimmed hats, and lovely mansions floated before her. She would ignore Jimmy Bryant then!

She smiled up at Rock. "How could I forget?" she asked dreamily.

Later she saw Mimi and Nancy go up to Jimmy themselves and ask for his autograph. Her ears burned while they chatted with him for a few minutes. She could tell they were talking about her because of the several glances they sent her way. She lifted her chin and resumed her animated conversation with Rock, pretending she had not seen a thing.

While Mama and Papa were bidding the Bryants good night and congratulating them on their son's success, she saw Jimmy deliberately hang back. Boldly she looked his way. But he gave no sign of recognition. Instead, he quickly picked up his guitar and, with the other two boys, left by a different door. Hurt and angry, she watched a crowd of fans follow him out.

The next morning she was awakened by a loud shriek. Sleepily she sat up just as Dixie flew into her room and turned on her bedside radio.

"My gosh, haven't you got 'Tune Time' on?" her pajama-clad sister cried, horrified. She flipped the dial so vigorously that she almost sent the small plastic intrument sliding to the floor. "They're playing 'Redwing Mountain.'"

Teddi forced a bored yawn.

"So what?" she mumbled and flopped back onto her pillow, rolling its softness about her head. Even so, the strains of Jimmy's song, and hers, could still be heard.

> "I was born on Redwing Mountain
> Seems a million years ago. . . ."

She sat up then. Dixie was sitting, feet under her, on her pale blue, satin-covered chair, a look of pure bliss covering her freckled face.

Ricky toddled in and pointed to the radio. "Yimmy!" he chortled.

It seemed that Jimmy was a favorite of everyone in her family—except her.

Oh, well, she might as well listen to his song, too. Taking Ricky up on the bed, she settled back. Before she knew it she was surprised to find herself enjoying and humming the mournful ballad.

It told of fictional incidents in the singer's childhood—happy times and sad. It told of his growing up and meeting a blue-eyed girl who became his true love. Then came the singing recital of their parting, when he left home to seek his fortune in the city. She promised to wait for him, and she waited for a long time. But, in the meantime, his interests wandered away from her and he failed to answer her letters. One day his fortunes worsened and he returned home, repentant. He found his blue-eyed sweetheart engaged to another. But, after a long time spent in proving his love had always been true, he won her back. The song ended with the girl renouncing her new love and marrying him.

In the last verse the young man vowed:

> "Now I'll stay on Redwing Mountain
> Nevermore shall I roam;
> From now on old Redwing Mountain
> Will be my beloved home."

It was pure corn. She had known it and so had Jimmy. "But what's wrong with corn?" he had asked on the afternoon they had written it.

As the last strains died away Dixie let out a long sigh.

"Just think, Jimmy Bryant on the radio," she said dreamily. Then she turned to Teddi and demanded, "How about joining my Jimmy Bryant fan club?"

"Okay," Teddi agreed.

"Otay," piped up Ricky.

"Good! Two new members!" Dixie said and skipped gaily back to her room.

While Ricky continued to play on her bed, Teddi leaned back and lost herself in deep thought. Jimmy Bryant, a recording star. It did not seem possible. Recording artists had always seemed unreal to Teddi. But Jimmy was an old friend, a special friend. And she was his certain girl.

Certain girl! Last night at the dance he had acted as though she didn't exist. She sat up so quickly that she upset two of Ricky's little plastic Indians with which he was playing. From now on she'd forget Jimmy Bryant existed, too.

She found that wasn't easy. All day Saturday the strains of "Redwing Mountain" and the song on its flip side, filled the house. Dixie had every available radio going full blast. She tuned in every disc jockey in town. It seemed as if every one of them was determined to make a hit of that record.

In spite of her determination to put Jimmy Bryant as far from her thoughts as possible, she kept hoping he would call. Perhaps just to say, "Hello, how did you like my secret?" But he didn't call. At the end of the day she wondered if she could forget him as easily as he seemed to have forgotten her.

It was Sunday morning when Papa made her resolve again that she *could* forget about Jimmy. Mr. Taylor grinned broadly over his newspaper at her and said, "Look who made the society page!"

"Who?" she asked, puzzled. Jimmy probably. He seemed to be getting all the publicity lately. But why would they put him on the society page?

"You."

"Where?" she squealed. "Let me see."

Papa folded the paper into a smaller square. Then he handed it to her. "There," he said.

Her eyes swept the headline of the article to which his broad finger pointed. HOSTESSES CHOSEN FOR PILGRIMAGE, it read. Then below, in smaller type, it continued, "Three popular and prominent young ladies will serve as guides at each of the six old homes to be shown to visitors."

There, looking as big as the biggest headline, was her name, Teddi Taylor. Together with Nancy Moore's and Mimi Martineaux's names, it stated that they were the three girls assigned to the Martineaux mansion. This was just what she had wanted!

Her excitement mounting, she read on. The article told all about the coming flower festival, and how it would be sponsored by merchants of the city. A queen would be selected, and she would ride in one of the many floats in the parade that would open the event. Prizes would be awarded for the most beautiful flower displays in city yards. The Pilgrimage was described as an essential part of the festival. It would give newcomers to the city, as well as residents, the opportunity to tour some of the lovely old homes that made up an important part of the city's heritage.

Teddi was ecstatic. This was just the beginning of the publicity for the festival. Other articles would appear in the paper, with pictures and announcements. There would be personal appearances on radio and television. She remembered that last year all the hostesses had been guests on a local evening program. They had looked lovely in their costumes. This year she would appear with them!

She sat up straight. Jimmy wasn't the only one in the public eye. In a few minutes the telephone would start ringing. Colfax Street neighbors would call to tell her they had seen her name in the paper and to congratulate her on the high honor she had received.

The telephone did ring and the call was for her. Viv's voice fairly bubbled over the wire.

"Say, have you been listening to the radio? Haven't they been giving Jimmy and his trio a big play? All the disc jockeys say his record is a surefire hit. Oh, I'm so proud of Jimmy! Aren't you, Certain Girl?"

Teddi gave the receiver a baleful look. She almost said, "Certain Girl, bah, humbug!" But instead she forced herself to say sweetly, "Oh, yes. Very proud."

Viv continued to rattle on about Jimmy and the trio and the record, and how excited everybody on Colfax Street was. She did not even mention seeing Teddi's name in the paper.

The excitement went on all week. With each passing day publicity on the record increased. Every disc jockey in the area, and later on in the state, played the record many times each day. The boys made personal appearances on radio programs in several nearby towns. That Saturday night they were featured on a local television show.

The Taylors, with Rock, watched the program eagerly.

"Aren't they scrumptious?" crowed Dixie for the thousandth time that week. Only minutes before she had announced that her Jimmy Bryant fan club now boasted a hundred members.

While the others agreed emphatically, Teddi sat silently, as though the boys on the screen were perfect strangers. During that whole week Jimmy had not called her once.

"And just think," Dave teased. "Our Teddi is known as Jimmy's certain girl."

"Hummmph!" Teddi flared and walked out of the room.

18

Opening Day

It was Sunday morning, the day before the opening of the festival. The whole Taylor family was examining closely a pictorial layout on the front page of the society section of the Holston *Times*. Several pictures had been taken at the old homes to be open for the Pilgrimage, with the hostesses for each attractively arranged on the lawns or porticoes. The most prominent picture on the page showed Teddi and Nancy and Mimi standing between the tall, white pillars of the Martineaux mansion.

"We'll need extra copies of this," Papa said with a proud grin. "Our out-of-town relations will want to see it."

Mama nodded. "I can think of some right now," she said. "Joe and his family, Emma and Lucille, and Tom. . . ."

Papa's blue eyes twinkled. "Those are your relations," he said. "I'm thinking of mine. . . . Mama and Papa, and Bo and Ella and. . . . Guess I'd better go downtown and get a dozen or so from the newsstand."

Teddi beamed. She was ecstatic. Just looking at the picture of her and Nancy and Mimi sent a thrill through her. She was really flying high!

Then the wind of remembrance blew away her happiness. It wouldn't last long, this new-found acceptance among the folks on the Hill. Back came every word of the conversation she had heard the evening before.

As usual Papa and Mama had been having their last cup of coffee in the kitchen before retiring. Teddi, in pajamas, had been on her way downstairs for a bedtime snack when Papa's words had halted her on the bottom step.

"I haven't had a nibble on those houses in Mountainside yet," he had said, his voice heavy with worry. "And I am in real need of some of the money I have tied up in them. If those houses don't sell soon, I'll have to sell this so I can meet the payments on those loans I made from the bank. In that case, we'll just have to move back to the house on Colfax Street."

Teddi had sunk, dismayed, onto the stairs. She hadn't wanted to eavesdrop, but she couldn't help overhearing the conversation.

Move out of this home? Oh, no! Even Mimi's resumed coldness could not squelch her feeling of being accepted by Nancy and Eddie and Rock and, yes, even Tess Graves! Tess had waved at her when, after the picture taking, all the hostesses had gathered at the Martineaux house for instructions in their duties at the old homes during the Pilgrimage. If a queen had acknowledged her presence Teddi couldn't have felt more flattered!

"Remember, all we have to do is sell that first house," Mama had said soothingly. "Once it sells, the others will soon follow. And I'm sure that will. . . ."

Teddi had waited to hear no more. She had fled, snackless, back to her own room. Why did life have to be so difficult? It seemed that when one problem was solved, another immediately popped up.

After the square dance at the Rec Hall, she had thought she and Mimi were on good terms. Then, when she and Nancy had gone to the Martineaux mansion to have their picture taken, Mimi had been cold and aloof again.

Her grandmother had greeted them warmly. The handsome, white-haired old lady had come out on the portico and half embraced them. "Ah, two of Mimi's charming young friends!" she had cried. "Come, Mimi, this is a happy time."

But Mimi had seemed to think it the worst of times. She had muttered a tight-lipped, "Hi, there," then clammed up. From then on she had acted as though she couldn't wait until the pictures were taken so she could go back into her shell again.

"It's the bad news from her parents," Mrs. Martineaux had whispered. "They wrote and said they were coming here for a few days. Now they find they can't make it. Mimi is terribly disappointed."

Teddi had sympathized with Mimi. Now she looked around the living room at her own family, thankful she didn't have *that* kind of problem.

Then, as though she thought Teddi's picture was giving her entirely too much attention, Dixie piped up, "Forgot to tell you. Mimi Martineaux told me she would go to the farm with us next Sunday! She wants to see ol' Cottonblossom."

Teddi's heart sank. Honestly, it seemed that at times, Dixie just didn't use common sense. She wanted to take Mimi out to that rundown old farm, where Grandpa would be in overalls and Grandma in apron and sunbonnet!

Then another thought made her feel better. When she had talked to Dixie, Mimi had been in her friendly mood. Now that she was her aloof self again she would probably call and say she couldn't go.

Teddi shrugged. What did it matter whether Mimi went to the farm or not? If that first house in Mountainside didn't sell soon, the Taylors wouldn't be living on the Hill much longer, anyway. Once back on Colfax Street, she wouldn't have to worry about what Mimi thought of the farm, her grandparents, or anything.

The telephone rang and Teddi's gloomy thoughts vanished. It was probably a Colfax Street neighbor calling to say he had seen the picture.

"It's for you, Miz Taylor," Elvira called from the hallway.

Mama hastened to answer the call. She was back in a few minutes, smiling happily.

"It was Mrs. Harris," she said. "Her brother called last night from Chicago. He will be in Holston in a day or so to look for a home. Mrs. Harris wanted to know if we would take him out to see the Mountainside houses Thursday morning." She looked anxiously at Papa. "Of course, I said we would."

"You were absolutely right in saying so!" Papa beamed.

Teddi, however, squirmed in embarrassment. She couldn't understand how Mama or Papa could think for a minute that Rock's parents would be interested in those Mountainside houses. While they were nice, they certainly weren't the kind the Baxters would want to live in.

Life was strange, she thought wryly. In many ways it was more simple, and sometimes more fun, on Colfax Street. Still, she didn't want to move back.

The telephone rang again, and this time the call was for her. Viv was on the line.

"What a perfectly scrumptious picture!" she glowed. "Though it doesn't do you justice, Teddi, believe me! Everybody says so. Oh, boy, you should see the folks here on Colfax Street! Everybody's running around showing it to neighbors who are on their way to show it to them! Gosh, how does it feel to be famous?"

It was good to hear from Viv! She always rejoiced in the good fortune of others without a trace of envy. It was nice to have a friend like Viv.

"Oh, I didn't think the picture was very good myself," Teddi replied casually.

"Well, I think it is just *grand!*" Viv was emphatic. "And you know what? It has caused almost as much excitement on Colfax Street as Jimmy's record!"

Teddi winced. Jimmy and his old record! He hadn't called her yet. But she wasn't going to let him or Viv or anybody else think that she cared, so she ignored that remark.

"Well, be watching for me in the parade tomorrow," she said gaily. "I'll be on the Pilgrimage float, and it is really pretty."

This was an understatement, she thought. She and Nancy had seen the float for the first time yesterday. Mrs. Harris had taken them to the old carriage house of one of the Women's Club members where the decorating committee was putting the finishing touches on it. She and Nancy had gasped at its beauty. And for good reason. In the center of the bed of a large truck, on a "lawn" of shredded green paper, stood a replica of the Martineaux mansion. Around it were tubs of crape myrtle in full bloom. Other tubs spilled their rich-hued blossoms among the white wrought-iron settees upon which the hostesses were to sit. Teddi had thrilled anew at being chosen to sit on that float with the other girls.

"Everybody on Colfax Street will be there watching," Viv promised enthusiastically. "That will be a treat none of us will want to miss."

Later that morning, at church and Sunday School, Teddi met others who congratulated her on how nice she looked in the picture. She didn't see Jimmy, although she had hoped she would. Jack Walker, however, was most attentive and flattering in his remarks. To her surprise he walked from the educational building into the church with her and sat beside her during the service.

Viv called again that afternoon. When Teddi casually mentioned that she hadn't seen Jimmy at church, Viv cried, "That's why I called you! His mom just called mine and said that Jimmy was in Nashville and she didn't expect him back until this afternoon. Seems he got a sudden call to go there and talk over a possible appearance of the trio on 'Western Roundup,' you know, that nationally televised program of country and folk music. Isn't it wonderful?"

"It certainly is!" Teddi replied, weakened by the significance of that announcement. An appearance of Jimmy and the trio on a nationwide network of television stations certainly meant that they were flying high. She added, not entirely in jest, "I'll bet when he comes back he won't even notice his old friends."

Jimmy had said she would change after moving to the Hill. Well, it would be Jimmy who wouldn't be the same after such an appearance with the trio.

"Oh, I don't think so!" Viv flew to his defense. "Jimmy's a pretty solid kid, you know."

"No, I didn't know," Teddi remarked.

The call ended on a rather cool note. Teddi felt a bit sheepish. It had been jealousy that had made her talk like she did, and she knew it. Why couldn't she be a booster like Viv? Why couldn't she say nice things about everybody, or nothing at all?

Late that afternoon her gaiety returned, however. Nancy and Eddie, Dave and Sybil, and she and Rock were lounging between dips around the pool. Again she felt herself a part of the life on the Hill. Viv and Jimmy seemed very remote, except when she thought how nice it would be if Jimmy would call her and tell her when he and the trio were going to appear on that Nashville program. But he didn't call.

The opening day of the festival dawned bright and clear. The streets of Holston looked their loveliest as carefully tended flower beds in yards and parks turned the town into a bower of beauty.

As Teddi climbed aboard the Pilgrimage float and took her place on one of the settees, she felt proud and happy. She had arrived at an exalted place in Holston social life, and she liked it.

As Viv had predicted, the neighbors of Colfax Street had turned out en masse to witness her triumph. On the way to Big Spring Park, where the parade formed, she had a good look at the gathering crowds. The Newbys were on one corner, right in the middle of several grinning soldiers. Mrs. Hart and her two younger children stood on another, and across the street from them were the Bryants. Here and there Teddi saw other familiar faces, as Papa had to drive slowly through the milling throng.

Would Jimmy be among them? Probably not. He was probably feeling too important to be on hand, for the morning paper had carried the news that the Jimmy Bryant trio would appear on "Western Roundup" three weeks from Saturday! No, she wouldn't see him here today.

Resolutely she put all thoughts of Jimmy from her mind. As the parade began its slow procession out of the park into the main streets she felt as bouncy as the high-stepping baton twirlers preceding the half-dozen school bands.

All along the way onlookers stood two or three deep. They were obvious about their admiration for the Pilgrimage float.

"It's prettier than the queen's float!" some of them cried.

"Prettiest one in the parade!" shouted others.

"Hi, Teddi!" someone yelled, and turning, Teddi saw Lyle and Viv waving at her from the curb.

She waved back happily.

"Atta girl, Teddi!" Turning, she saw Mr. Newby on the other side of the street, looking at her with a wide grin on his deeply tanned face.

"My, isn't she pretty?" Mrs. Newby cried shrilly.

A titter sounded around Teddi. Were the other hostesses having fun at her expense? She hadn't heard any of the crowd yell at *them*. Was it because their friends wouldn't act so common?

She shrank back, hoping Mr. Robinson wouldn't see her. But he did—and he cried out and waved at her. So did two of Viv's older brothers. She had to wave back.

"Quite a fan club," one of the hostesses remarked, and Teddi found herself torn between embarrassment and pleasure.

She still hadn't seen Jimmy, though she had continually scanned the crowd for him. She wouldn't admit it, but seeing him would have made up for any of the other shortcomings in her day.

Then she saw him, standing in the doorway of the Acme Drugstore. He recognized her, she was sure of that. Should she give him a tiny, ladylike nod, and then wave with her white-gloved hand? It wouldn't embarrass her if he did holler at her. She could turn to the other girls and say, "That's Jimmy Bryant." They wouldn't snicker at that news.

But, if she nodded and waved, would he wave back? It would be embarrassing if he didn't, for somehow she felt that others were observing the little tableaux.

Her chance passed swiftly.

Why didn't I wave? she thought, miserable for a moment. Then her spirits rose. He *had* come to see her.

There were Papa and Mama, beaming proudly at their girl. Dixie and Rick and Dave caught her eye to let her know they were proud of her, too. Grandma and Grandpa Taylor, who had come in to town just to see the parade, beamed up at her.

After the parade was over, the hostesses, still in their costumes, walked from Big Spring Park to the homes where they would spend the rest of that day and all the rest of the days of the week. Even the walk was like a parade, with folks watching them in open admiration.

Mrs. Martineaux asked Teddi and Nancy to stay for lunch. It was eaten in a sun-drenched summerhouse behind the mansion. Teddi had never seen Mimi looking so sad and lonely.

Soon the sightseers began coming to the mansion. Teddi enjoyed taking them around the house and grounds, answering questions, and explaining various objects of historical interest.

When the day was over, Teddi fairly skipped home. It had been a wonderful day. And there were five more days to follow!

The minute she went through the front door of her home she knew something was wrong. Only Elvira was there, a solemn look in her dark eyes.

"Your grandpa, Miss Teddi," she said quietly. "He took real sick all of a sudden this afternoon. Yo' papa and mama and grandma just carried him to the hospital."

19

Coming Storm

Like the interior of a cathedral, the large entry hall of the Martineaux mansion seemed to have a quieting effect on those who entered it. They walked on tiptoe and spoke in hushed whispers. But would it quiet Viv? Teddi wondered anxiously when she saw Viv and Ruby and Carol approaching the portico.

She was back on duty the next morning. Grandpa's condition wasn't serious, but he would have to stay under observation in the hospital for a week or ten days. And that brought on another complication, as far as Teddi was concerned.

"Mama, you can't stay on the farm by yourself," Papa had told Grandma firmly. "You must stay here with us. I don't want to have to worry about you and Papa, too."

It had taken quite a bit of persuading on his part, before Grandma would agree.

"I feel like a fish out of water when I'm in town," the old lady had complained. But she had gone with Papa to close up the house at Redwing Crossing and get some extra clothes.

Teddi had watched in dismay as Grandma and her old-fashioned suitcase entered the stylish big house on the Hill.

The old lady looked more countryish than usual, it had seemed to Teddi, in her plain, faded clothes. Teddi had hoped that none of the neighbors had witnessed her coming.

In the last week or so Teddi had been relieved to see a change in Mama. Mrs. Taylor had taken to wearing good "casual" clothes around the house. And she had gone to a hair stylist for a new hairdo, too. It was surprising how much Mama's appearance had been changed.

But Grandma often said, "You can't teach an old dog new tricks," and that applied to old ladies, too, it seemed. Papa's mama kept right on wearing her wispy white hair in a bun on top of her head. And Teddi was certain she wore an apron everywhere except to church.

"If she wears one of her old sunbonnets out in the yard here, I think I'll die," she had thought fiercely after Grandma had been settled in the downstairs bedroom.

This very morning, however, as she had left home for the Martineaux house she had spied Grandma out in the yard planting flowers. "The yard looks so bare," the old lady had said while eating her oatmeal breakfast. She had been doing her planting on the sunny side of the house, and she had been wearing a narrow-brimmed sunbonnet!

Teddi had quickly fled up the street toward the Martineaux house, thinking thankfully, *I'm glad there aren't any sightseers coming to our house!*

Now she had Viv to contend with—noisy, boisterous Viv, who would waste no time letting everybody know that they were old friends. She couldn't flee, for Viv had seen her first.

"Hi, there, Teddi, old pal!" Viv yelled and waved at her. "You gonna show us through the place? It better be good. We paid thirty-five cents apiece for our tickets, you know."

She laughed heartily at her own joke, and Teddi was sure

she could have been heard downtown. It certainly attracted the attention of other sightseers, especially two German-speaking ladies who had just come upon the portico. The wives of imported personnel at the government arsenal. Teddi knew they were classifying all American teen-agers as noisy, unmannerly, and rowdy. Their eyes and low, disapproving clucks said so.

"I'll take Viv and Carol and Ruby through in a hurry," Teddi vowed grimly. When the girls drew close, she said softly, "I think you will like what you see. The house is really lovely."

She hoped Viv noticed her low, modulated tone of voice, and her choice of words. Her manner of speaking had changed, she was sure, since she had moved to the Hill.

The regal old house seemed to quiet Viv a bit. At least, as she stepped into the high-ceilinged hall with its great spiral staircase at one end, she lowered her voice to breathe, "Wow! Some dump!"

Carol and Ruby murmured something similar. But they had never been as noisily talkative as Viv; around her they rarely had a chance to be.

Feeling better now that Viv's manner and voice were more decorous, Teddi took them on the full tour. She showed them everything with as much pride as if she had been mistress of the place herself.

She thought the girls were properly impressed until they were out on the portico and ready to leave. Then Viv, resuming her usual loud tone of voice, remarked, "It's nice, I suppose, but I wouldn't give two cents to live in it."

Teddi turned amazed eyes on her Colfax Street friend. "Why not?" she demanded.

Viv shrugged her plump shoulders. "It would be like living in a museum or haunted house," she said. "Every time you turned around you'd expect a ghost to pop out of one of those dark corners."

Carol and Ruby nodded vigorously in agreement.

"And not one single beat-up sofa or chair to flop on," complained Carol, though not so loudly.

"Everything just seems to holler 'mustn't touch,'" added Ruby.

Viv took a stick of gum out of her purse. Unwrapping it carefully, she put the paper in a small container placed on the portico for that purpose.

"I'll take my house on Colfax Street any old time," she said, popping the gum into her mouth. "Not so elegant, maybe, but a lot more inviting and comfortable."

"You said it!" Carol was emphatic. "I guess being poor isn't all bad."

"It certainly isn't," said Ruby.

"Well, so long, Teddi, old kid."

"Good-bye."

Teddi turned to greet an elderly man and his wife who had just appeared, tickets in hand. As she did she noticed, a few feet away, Mrs. Pierre Martineaux sitting stiffly on one of the white chairs. She had heard every word the girls had said; this was plain from her manner which was not really angry, but thoughtfully frowning.

"Well!" Teddi heard her say as she rose and started back into the house. "So that is what the young folks think of Mimi's home. Something simply will have to be done about it."

Tears of chagrin sprang to Teddi's eyes. Viv had done it again; she had simply ruined her chances of becoming friendly with Mimi and her aristocratic grandmother. Mrs. Martineaux had surely meant that, from now on, Mimi would have nothing to do with Teddi Taylor and her rowdy friends.

Well, from now on Teddi Taylor wasn't going to have anything to do with those friends, either. They simply did not fit into her new life, and she was going to stop her efforts to make them fit in.

Then a tiny voice inside spoke up. *Yesterday during the parade you were happy to see these same friends looking up at you with admiring eyes.*

But that was yesterday. The past belongs to the past and is best forgotten.

While she was at home during her lunch hour Viv called. "Know something?" she bubbled. "Jimmy and the trio are going to be on the 'Western Roundup' *this* Saturday night!"

"But I thought. . . ."

"It would be a couple of weeks yet? So did they. But it seems another singing group scheduled to appear this Saturday night had to cancel out because of sickness or something. So Jimmy got a wire this morning asking if he and the boys could fill in. Naturally he said 'yes,' and right quick, too. He and the boys are leaving tonight on the bus. Rehearsals start tomorrow. Isn't that something?"

"It certainly is," Teddi replied, and the enthusiasm in her voice was genuine. Some of her Colfax Street friends were all right, she decided—especially Jimmy.

She couldn't understand, however, why *he* hadn't called her and given her this good news. In the old days she would have been the first to know. She was more sorry than ever that she had missed him the other afternoon when he had delivered groceries to her house. Elvira had said, after some prodding, that he hadn't even mentioned her name.

It was a good thing she had a friend like Viv in the old neighborhood. How else would she hear what was going on? The rest of them seemed to shy away from calling her and giving her such information. Viv wasn't really so bad, except at certain times and places.

She could call Jimmy right now and congratulate him. That could be the wedge opening up their friendship again. She was halfway through dialing his number when her finger stopped. Again she saw him in the doorway of that drugstore. He had been fully aware of her on that float, and he hadn't waved.

Her call now would make him think she was chasing him! That she was eager to share his ever enlarging place in the sun.

"I don't need him to make myself noticed," she said with satisfaction. "After all, I'm getting plenty of attention as a hostess at the Martineaux mansion."

She let the receiver click back into place. *Something is wrong,* she thought miserably, *when I can't call up Jimmy and wish him well.* But what was it?

A downward glance revealed a thread hanging from the hem of her hoopskirted dress. *I'd better cut that,* she thought. *If I pull it I might take out the hem.*

She started down the upstairs hall toward Mama's room. Entering it, she looked around. Where were the scissors? The room had been darkened against the fierce rays of the morning sun. In spite of air conditioning Mama usually drew the shades to keep rugs and upholstered furniture from fading. Teddi let up one shade, opening up before her an excellent view of the front walk and lawn. Looking down, she gasped at what she saw. There was Mrs. Pierre Martineaux approaching the Taylor front door with small, clicking steps!

What had caused this sudden visit of their aristocratic neighbor? she thought in panic. Was it something she had done wrong? Or Dixie? Did the remarks Viv had made that morning have something to do with it?

While these thoughts whirled in her mind, a new one added to her woe. Who would greet Mrs. Martineaux? Mama had gone back to the hospital and Papa had returned to work.

Teddi tried to pull herself together and face the situation calmly. Whatever the occasion for the visit, it must be met with the proper decorum and respect. And she was the only one to do it.

Then, suddenly, she turned cold. Grandma was downstairs! When Teddi had last seen her, she had been in the kitchen helping Elvira and keeping an eye on Ricky.

One thing was certain—she must not let Grandma get to the front door ahead of her! If that happened. . . . She shuddered. Grandma's inevitable apron would look dowdy beside the sleekly fitted, dark silk print frock of their visitor. Her wispy bun would be a great contrast to the regally upswept, blue-tinted coiffure of the grande dame of Holston society. Her thick-soled shoes would clump awkwardly beside the tiny, patent, spike-heeled pumps of Mimi's grandmother.

Teddi tried to move, but her feet seemed frozen to the floor. Then, with real effort she regained the use of them and raced downstairs. She hoped desperately that the roar of the dishwasher had drowned out the tinkle of the doorbell. At the bottom of the steps she stopped in dismay. Grandma was already at the door!

"Well, howdy, howdy!" The elder Mrs. Taylor's high-pitched voice was cordial. "Lan' sakes, it's good to see a neighbor. I was just tellin' my boy last ev'nin' that folks around here don't seem as neighborly as the ones at Redwing Crossing." She laughed shrilly. "I'll have to eat crow now, won't I?"

Mrs. Martineaux's low, modulated laughter came to Teddi. She cringed at the difference in their manner of speaking.

"Oh, I have meant to call a number of times," the mistress of

Martineaux mansion said. "But it seemed that something came up every time to prevent it."

"That is the very reason I don't like livin' in town," Grandma chattered on. "Rush, rush, rush! I declare, folks don't take the time to eat and sleep hardly, much less go visitin'. Cain't we set out on the porch? I declare, I just cain't abide air conditioning."

"Why, certainly; I'm not very fond of it myself."

"Well, I'm glad to hear of somebody else who don't cotton to all these new-fangled modern conveniences. I'd about as soon fry as freeze. Care for a fan?"

Oh, no, Teddi moaned to herself, knowing well that Mrs. Martineaux was agreeing with Grandma just to be polite. The thought of anyone offering the aristocratic lady a cardboard fan on a stick, with advertising on it, made her positively sick. Why, one had to go miles out in the country to even find one of those turn-of-the-century items!

She heard the door close and the voices recede, so she knew Grandma and their visitor were out on the portico. She crept into the living room and discreetly peeked out through the big front window. There were the two old ladies—sitting on a settee chattering away and wielding their fans. At least Grandma was chattering. Even Papa said that nobody could outtalk his mama, and Papa was right.

Oh, dear, Teddi thought miserably as she made her way back to the enclosed patio. The Taylor family might just as well move back to Colfax Street. A beautiful home and a swimming pool could not make up for a grandma like hers.

She didn't hear Grandma come back into the house. A few minutes later, however, she heard her declare, "My, that Mrs. Martineaux is a fine old woman. We had a real nice visit."

Teddi could stand it no longer. She jumped up and ran into

the kitchen. "Well, I'm glad you enjoyed her visit because she will never be likely to call here again!" she cried, then ran back toward the stairs.

She saw a look of hurt pass over the wrinkled, kindly old face.

"I don't care!" she cried fiercely when, in her own room, she picked up her comb and ran it quickly through her hair. "It's true! It's true! Why didn't she stay in the country where she belongs!"

And she said that loud enough for Grandma to hear, too.

A glance at the clock on her desk told her it was one thirty and time to be back at her hostess job. Down the stairs she went, hoping not to see Grandma. But she did catch a glimpse of the old lady moving around in the downstairs bedroom.

She was miserable all afternoon. She shouldn't have said what she had to Grandma. But the whole thing was Grandma's fault. Why hadn't Grandma realized that she couldn't cope with someone like Mrs. Pierre Martineaux and excused herself. Then Mrs. Martineaux would have spoken briefly to Teddi and called another time. Now that Mama had improved her appearance, she would have made a good impression.

Oh, Grandma had certainly fixed things for her all right!

She did not see Mrs. Martineaux the rest of the afternoon. Mimi's grandmother was plainly avoiding her, and for good reason. Mimi spoke to her only once, and seemed more cool and distant. Even Nancy acted aloof. Mrs. Martineaux had lost no time telling her granddaughter all about the queer old creature at the Taylor home and, of course, Mimi had relayed the story to Nancy.

When the Martineaux house closed its doors to tourists that afternoon Teddi began her slow, reluctant trip home. She was so lost in her troubles that she did not notice the huge black

clouds billowing across the mountaintop until she was almost
in her own yard.

When she did notice, it was only for a moment. She knew
that soon the sky would blacken, then open up to let loose a
torrent of rain. Such storms were frequent around Holston.
Right now the clouds were no blacker than her mood, she
thought miserably.

Elvira, as usual, was busy in the kitchen. "Where's everybody?" Teddi asked her crossly.

Elvira turned to her, a look of real concern on her face. "Well,
yo' ma ain't back from the hospital, and yo' pa ain't in from
work. Dixie is over at the Moores' and Ricky is upstairs
asleep. . . . And I'm plumb worrit about yo' grandma."

"For goodness' sake, why? Isn't she in her room?"

"No, she ain't. 'Bout half hour ago she flew through here
like a ghost was after her. She clumb into that old truck of
yo' pa's and tuck off. She mumbled somethin' 'bout havin' to
go back to the farm." Elvira looked out the window over the
sink and shook her head. "An' with a storm comin' up."

Terror clutched Teddi. She knew what Elvira meant;
Grandma could be in real trouble if the storm overtook her.
Once outside Holston, the road to Redwing Crossing was
lonely, winding over and around hills and ridges and across a
creek that doubled back several times. Because of her arthritis
the old lady would have difficulty coping with such emergen-
cies as trees blown across the road, washed out bridges, and
landslides. And such things happened frequently during storms
in this area.

It had been her fault. She alone had driven Grandma out into
the storm.

"Ain't stayin' where I ain't wanted," she could almost hear
Grandma saying.

Wind flicked around the corner of the house. Leaves, so still during the hot afternoon, began to flutter ominously. Thunder boomed like a distant cannon, while lightning streaked across the peak of Redwing Mountain. The storm was fast approaching, and it was going to be a bad one.

20

Head in the Clouds

Storm warnings had been out since noon—mild at first, then increasingly foreboding. Tornadic winds would move into the area by late afternoon, they said, bringing rain and possibly hail.

Teddi had first heard the weather reports on the radio at home while waiting out the visit of Mrs. Martineaux. She had heard them later on a transistor set carried by a girl touring the mansion.

She, like other native residents of Holston, had paid little attention to them, although some of the newcomers whom she guided through the house had seemed worried. She had assured them that such forecasts were common in the area and that the dangerous storms which were predicted usually fizzled out into mild ones. Tornadoes had occurred around Holston, she had said. But they usually veered away from the city itself because of its location in a valley surrounded by mountains. Only occasionally did the tip of a funnel dip into the city and cause damage.

Had she ever seen a tornado? one frightened lady had asked. Then Teddi had told of the tornado she had seen skip over town with its funnel looking like the tail of a giant kite. Had she been scared? No, Papa had told her there was no reason to be.

She was scared now. Grandma was out in an area beyond the valley, where tornadoes often did hit. The old lady was there because of her granddaughter's thoughtless words, spoken in the heat of anger. Teddi's head throbbed as feelings of guilt pounded at her consciousness with the force of sledge hammers.

If only she could take back those words! Nobody's esteem, not that of a thousand Mrs. Martineaux's was worth one little hurt to Grandma. Why did such a realization always come too late? There wasn't a thing she could do to help Grandma. Or was there? A possibility came to her, a faint one. She ran to the telephone and dialed the Harrises' number.

As she had hoped, Rock answered. The words fairly tumbled out as she told him her problem. He gave a nervous little laugh. "Gosh, Teddi, I wouldn't want to try driving in a storm like the one I see coming up. Besides, I don't have a car because Aunt Eileen drove off in it an hour or so ago." A short hesitation followed before he added, "I wouldn't worry about the old lady. She is probably used to worse problems than this." He seemed a little relieved that he couldn't help her.

"Thanks, anyhow," Teddi said with a little sob, and hung up.

Should she call Papa or Mama? If she did, her part in the drama would have to be told. But was this the time to be thinking of herself? No! She was looking up the number of the hospital when she heard the back door slam.

"Elvira, you pick the darndest times to phone in a hurry-up grocery order." A familiar and, oh, so welcome voice sounded teasingly from the kitchen.

"Jimmy!" she breathed thankfully. She sped down the stairs toward the kitchen.

On the bottom step she stopped abruptly. This wasn't the old Jimmy, the Jimmy of whom she could ask a favor anytime and have it granted if it was at all possible! This was the new Jimmy, the recording star. She heard the thump of a box of groceries as he set it down on the kitchen table.

"Wow, this storm is going to be a lulu!" he added.

He *sounded* like the old Jimmy. Old or new, what did it matter, anyway? Grandma's welfare was at stake. Chin up, she rushed into the kitchen.

Jimmy turned when he heard her come in. "Well, what do you know?" he asked coolly. *He's changed,* she thought with sinking heart. "Long time, no see."

No, she couldn't do it. She couldn't ask a favor of this Jimmy. After all, she had her pride. Pride? What about the danger to Grandma? Hadn't it been her pride that had created this awful situation?

Teddi gulped.

"Too long, don't you think?" she said humbly. Then, turning beseeching eyes on Jimmy, she told him quickly of Grandma's danger, and the reason for it.

"It was all my fault, Jimmy," she wailed. "If only I hadn't said what I did to her! I can't take it back but I would like to help her if I could. I can't drive and, and. . . ."

"You want me to go out and catch up with her?" Jimmy's voice quickly changed from coolness to warmth.

"If only you would, Jimmy! With you at the wheel there would be little to worry about."

The tight lines about Jimmy's mouth relaxed. "Well, I wouldn't say that," he said softly. "But I'll do the best I can." His gaze flicked out the window. The black clouds scudding over Redwing Mountain were plainly visible. "And I'd better get going if I'm going to catch Grandma before this storm breaks."

He was on his way to the door when Teddi stopped him. "I'm going with you," she said firmly.

Turning, he warned, "You'd better not. Your folks'll worry when they find out where you are."

She eyed him levelly. "So will yours. And remember, I'm the one to blame for Grandma's being out there."

He shrugged, his face more grim. "Suit yourself, but let's get a move on." Out the door they went.

Elvira watched with wide-eyed concern as they ran for the pickup truck in the driveway. She moaned anxiously when the wind almost swept them off their feet.

Teddi didn't wonder this time what the neighbors thought about her climbing into the truck with BRYANTS' GROCERIES AND MEATS printed on both sides. The truck was a welcome sight now.

Jimmy set the engine roaring, spun the truck around, and sent it down the driveway out into Holly Tree Lane. Leaves swirled before them as they slipped down the Hill. Headlights of other cars switched on as their occupants hurried home before the storm struck.

She and Jimmy, she realized with growing concern, were just going out into it.

Grimly intent on his driving, Jimmy turned the truck into Governor's Drive. Picking up speed, they made their way rapidly toward the outskirts of town where County Line Road turned off.

A branch ripped away from a tree on the lawn of a two-story house and sailed right over the truck. It smashed loudly into a store window across the street.

Teddi flinched. Knuckles white from holding the wheel so tightly, Jimmy looked straight ahead. Teddi wished he would talk. *If he would just say something,* she thought, *it would help banish this churning misery inside me.* Her guilt weighed more heavily than ever upon her. It was all her fault that they were out here in this lashing prelude to the storm. It was all her fault that Grandma was out in it.

It seemed silly now to have been so concerned over Mrs. Martineaux's opinion of her grandma. In her way Grandma might be a little different. But then, wasn't everybody?

After they had found Grandma safe—and they must—she would never be ashamed of the old lady again. Never! Nor of Mama or Papa or Dixie or Viv or any of her other Colfax Street friends. They were what they were and so was she. From now on she wouldn't pretend anything else. If anybody on the Hill, or elsewhere, wanted to be her friend, he or she would have to take her as she was, humble background and all. If they didn't, well, friendship built on pretensions was a flimsy thing, anyway, always having to be bolstered with lies and evasions.

A flash of lightning revealed the abandoned filling station and pile of automobile skeletons that marked the turn into County Line Road. The truck swerved and bounced onto the old road.

Teddi's heart jumped into her throat. What a lonely stretch of road this was, stretching through a flatland of worn-out cotton fields before it disappeared into the foothills of the Cumberlands. Travel on it was sparse.

Somewhere Grandma was steering that old truck of Papa's, fleeing from a thoughtless, heartless granddaughter. The thought sickened her.

Jimmy leaned over the wheel in an effort to peer through

the clouds of red dust blowing off the dried-clay fields and dodge the limbs of trees, a roll of wire fencing, rusty, rotted fenders and other loose parts from the pile of dead cars which were blowing across the road.

"Look out for Grandma in the ditch on your side," Jimmy said tersely. "I'll keep an eye out for her over here."

This brought Teddi up straight.

"Oh, I hope she hasn't run the truck into one of those ditches!" she cried.

"I hope so, too," Jimmy replied grimly. "But with visibility practically zero, she could have."

He slowed the truck to a crawl. Teddi strained her eyes in an effort to catch a glimpse of any truck that might have slipped into one of the deep drainage ditches along the sides of the road. During heavy rains she knew that they, as well as the creek a half mile away, overflowed and flooded the flat-lands.

The truck bumped into a tire blown onto the road and banged over a rusty fender. Teddi, her nerves taut already, stifled a scream. Each one of those objects could have been Grandma out on the road walking for help!

Big drops on the windshield told them the rain had started— rain that quickly turned to hail as big as marbles. Through it Teddi caught a blurred glimpse of two cows huddled together and a horse with hanging head.

Then, as quickly as it had started, the hail stopped. An ominous quiet descended over the truck, roadside, and fields. An eerie greenish light appeared all around. Then came a roar like a freight train approaching.

Jimmy stopped the truck. "Roll down your window!" he yelled. "Tornado!"

Teddi nodded numbly. She saw the twister coming, its long,

trunklike cone reaching down from the frightening clouds overhead.

Terrified, she rolled down the window. The suction of the wind from a tornado could cause even a house to explode if it was shut up tightly.

She and Jimmy dropped to the floor. Faces flat on the seat, they held hands, hearing the roar become louder and louder until it seemed as if the whole world was filled with it.

The car shook violently. Then, suddenly, it stopped and the roar subsided. There was a strange, eerie silence.

Unbelieving, Teddi and Jimmy straightened up and looked out. The atmosphere was so clear they could see for miles.

The tornado was still visible, miles away, dangling its cone of destruction. It had surely been headed for them. Then, in the inexplicable way of the fearsome things, it had changed its course and swerved away.

It had touched earth, briefly, in a grove of trees several miles away, where a dozen or more huge trees were now uprooted and strewn about.

Both Teddi and Jimmy knew that the tornado *could* turn and come back their way.

"Let's get out of here!" Jimmy cried as they scrambled back onto the seat. Soon they were shooting off down the road as though it were as straight and smooth as a four-lane highway. Within minutes they had reached the comparative safety of the hills.

Nowhere along the way did they see Grandma. What could have become of her? Teddi's anxiety increased.

They reached Redwing Crossing at dusk. The storm had not touched it. The truck rumbled down the main street and across a tumbling creek until it reached the comfortable farm home of Mr. Taylor's parents.

"There's the truck!" Joyfully Teddi pointed to the ancient vehicle standing beside the house. "Grandma made it here after all."

They jumped out of the grocery truck and ran toward the kitchen at the rear of the house. On the porch they saw Grandma bending over, a bowl of milk in her hands, feeding a mother cat and her kittens.

Straightening up, the old lady almost dropped the bowl in surprise. "Lan' sakes, am I seeing ghosts?" she cried.

"No, Grandma, we're real!" Teddi cried happily. She ran to the thin, bent figure and hugged and kissed her until it seemed both would be dissolved in the tears. Her relief at seeing Grandma safe was so great that she babbled almost hysterically about how sorry she was for what she had said.

"Now, now." Grandma patted her fondly on the cheek and changed the subject. "I know you young 'uns are about starved. I'll go right in and fix you a bite."

Teddi struggled to get control of her emotions. She felt a bit shamefaced at baring them before Jimmy. Then she realized that he had discreetly gone back to the truck for his jacket. When he returned they went into the kitchen together and helped Grandma. Soon a stack of sandwiches, a plate of sliced tomatoes, and tall glasses of iced tea sat temptingly on the checked cloth that covered the round table by the window.

It was so nice to sit beside Jimmy in this old-fashioned, homey room, Teddi thought, without having to wonder what he thought of it. It was easy to see he was right at home. His relaxed, smiling face told her that.

After saying the blessing, Grandma smiled at them and said, "Help yourself. And there's ice cream in the freezer for dessert." She pointed to the big white appliance sitting in the pantry off the kitchen. "If I'd known I was having company I'd have baked one of my dried apple pies I have frozen in there."

She had made that last remark, Teddi knew, just to show off her freezer. The old lady was proud of it, and Teddi was grateful that with Jimmy she didn't have to feel ashamed of that pride. He knew how hard it was for some folks to acquire such possessions. It had been only a year ago that his folks had been able to afford a freezer.

Teddi glowed with contentment.

"This is plenty, Grandma," she said. "And everything looks so good."

"You can say that again," Jimmy agreed with a grin as he took a sandwich off the big plate and put it on his own. "Just looking at it makes me remember that I'm half starved."

Teddi was hungry, too. She took a sandwich and made a neat diagonal cut across it before she began to eat. It was peanut butter and jelly, her favorite.

While they ate, Grandma talked.

"Lan' sakes, I don't see why you got so upset when you found me gone and thought you must follow me," she scolded gently. "I'd never have gone out if I hadn't been mighty sure I could outrun the storm. All I caught was a little of the wind."

"We caught quite a bit," Jimmy said wryly, but he said nothing about how near the tornado had come to them. Teddi appreciated his tact, for she knew how upset Grandma would have been if told how close they had been to real danger.

"I just happened to remember," Grandma went on, "that I hadn't left anything out for Tabby to eat, everything being so upset and all. So I decided to come back and see about her and take care of a few other things around here."

The old lady lifted the top slice of bread off her cheese

sandwich and added more mustard. Her eyes were on Teddi as she continued softly, "Course, I didn't like what you said to me." Teddi lowered her eyes in shame. "Then I got to thinkin' that sometimes it's the truth that hurts most. I'm not in the same class as Mrs. Martineaux and, fact is, I felt pretty uncomfortable when I opened the door and saw her standin' there. But I thought I would do as best I could, as there weren't anybody else there to greet her."

She poured more tea for Jimmy and asked if he wanted more ice.

"Not now, thank you," he replied, looking uncomfortable at being in on such a private conversation.

"But I never took no offense," Grandma went on briskly. "I know there comes a time when all young'uns have a poor opinion of their elders." She chuckled. "Law, I did the same thing when I was young."

Jimmy winked at Teddi then, showing her that he, too, had similar troubles sometimes. Teddi's spirits began to rise.

"Spite of everything, though, me'n Mrs. Martineaux got along fine. She was soon tellin' me how worried she is about Minnie. . . ."

"Mimi," Teddi said smilingly.

"Well, seems she thinks Meemee don't mix as she should with other young folks. Something about the girl's ma and pa being on the go all the time, leavin' Meemee in boarding schools so much that the girl feels they don't care about her at all. This makes Meemee kinda touchy on the subject of parents, especially her own. When one of the kids calls attention to the fact that she isn't living with her folks, she feels blue for days. So, rather than run the risk of bein' hurt, Meemee avoids young folks much of the time."

Teddi gulped, remembering how Mimi had clammed up

when Viv had brought up the subject of her parents. She knew now that Dixie had been right in suspecting the truth about her withdrawn manner. Dixie probably never mentioned Mimi's parents to her, which was why the older girl preferred her company.

Grandma spooned sugar into her tea and stirred it vigorously. "It seems right now the poor girl feels worse'n usual. Her parents wrote and told her they were comin' to Holston for a few days before goin' on to Europe. Meemee was really lookin' forward to showin' everybody that she really has a ma and pa. Now it seems they can't come by." Grandma shook her head sadly. "Yes, sir, that old woman is real worrit about the girl. Seems she brought her here so she wouldn't have to go to another boarding school, and now she wonders if she did the right thing after all. She said the only time Meemee has seemed to enjoy herself while here was when she went to a square dance with you folks." Grandma looked at Teddi over her spectacles. "Recollect?"

Teddi's eyes sparkled at the news. "Yes, I certainly do, Grandma!"

Grandma nodded with pleasure. "Well, now she seems to think that another such dance might help matters some, get Meemee acquainted with more young folks. So Mrs. Martineaux thought she would like to hold one in that big old house of hers where she says there's a ballroom as big as a barn. She says it's about time things livened up around there anyway, that it's too much like a museum for a young girl to live in."

Teddi almost choked. Those were Viv's words! She had certainly been wrong about Mrs. Martineaux's reaction to them. She had been wrong about so many things!

"Well, she came down to your house, Teddi, to see if you and your folks and friends would help her with the affair. She thought you could supply her with a list of young folks to invite, and the name of that caller and. . . ."

"Art Blake," Jimmy smiled. Teddi was glad somebody was thinking straight. Her thoughts were muddled. "He'll go anywhere he can get a square together."

Grandma turned to him. "And she says Meemee is crazy over that record of yours and wanted to know if I thought you and the boys would come and sing songs and such during the evenin'."

Jimmy laughed. "I think we can manage."

Jimmy Bryant's trio singing and playing at the Martineaux house! But then weren't they recording and television stars? Television stars? "Jimmy!" Teddi cried in horror. "You were supposed to go to Nashville tonight to start rehearsals for that television program! Had you forgotten?"

Jimmy shook his head. "Hardly," he said. "I thought we might be back in time to catch the bus. It doesn't leave until ten fifteen."

Just then the telephone jangled.

They both heard Grandma say, "Why, yes, Tate, they are here, as frisky as a couple of rabbits in a carrot patch."

Papa started talking then, and they could tell by Grandma's worried nods and replies that he was telling her a bridge was out, roads were flooded, and trees down everywhere.

A look of concern flashed across Jimmy's face. Teddi felt miserable when Grandma turned and said, "Your papa says both of you must stay here until morning."

"Oh, Jimmy," Teddi cried softly. "I'm so sorry."

Jimmy shrugged, but she could tell he felt badly about not being able to make the date in Nashville. "I'll send a wire," he said quickly, "telling those in charge of rehearsals that I'll be a day late because of the storm."

Then he turned to Teddi and comforted her. "Don't you worry about it. It couldn't be helped. Anyway, there are some things more important than being a big shot, and Grandma is one of them." Grinning, he added, "My head may be in the clouds, but my feet are still on the ground—I hope."

21

Time Will Tell

The square dance was going to be the gayest affair held in the Martineaux mansion since Mimi's great-grandfather had honored his prize-winning cow, Jersey Sue. The story of that long-ago affair was well known in Holston. A reception and ball had been held to honor the cow when she had returned from the World's Columbian Exposition in Chicago. There she had been recognized as the world's champion milk producer. Then, as now, the lawn and stately old house were lit up like it was Christmas.

Then, as now, too, the entertainment would come fresh from triumphs in Nashville.

Teddi was as happy as she could be under the circumstances. *Almost* everything had turned out well since she and Jimmy had set off ahead of the tornado for Grandma's place at Redwing Crossing. Grandpa was improving, and Jimmy had managed, by flying, to join the trio the next day in time for rehearsals for the big show. The results had been a highly successful act.

All the Taylors had sat entranced for an hour before the television set that Saturday evening. Grandpa had been sent home, and was there with Grandma. Dixie was curled up in a big chair with Ricky squirming out of her lap to Grandma's and then back again. Rock had been there, and Nancy and Eddie and Sybil and Mimi.

"And don't say anything about her folks!" Dixie had whispered fiercely as Mimi had come in shyly.

Mama had made a big occasion of it. She had set bowls of popcorn and potato chips and plates of sandwiches and cookies on the table in the family room. For half an hour before show time they had sat and nibbled while they waited for it to begin.

Halfway through the show Jimmy and his trio had been presented. Ricky had yelled, "Yimmy!" then had settled back and enjoyed the performance along with the others.

Jimmy did especially well, it had seemed to them. On the screen he had projected the image of a bashful boy completely overwhelmed by his success. He had never been in better voice nor had his fingers ever been more nimble on the guitar.

The applause of the studio audience had been thundering, especially after their rendition of "Redwing Mountain."

The applause around the Taylor set had been thundering, too. Everyone was very proud of the local boys who had made good in the big time. So were all the other folks in Holston.

Teddi had not applauded. She had just sat numbly, while goose pimples had welled up all over her. It was just too fantastic! Jimmy Bryant and the trio he had formed were being featured on a nationally televised show! Could the boy in the center be the same Jimmy Bryant she had known since they were toddlers? The one with whom she had gone to square dances at the Rec Hall? The one who had kissed her on the cheek and called her his certain girl? She had closed her eyes dreamily. Of course, it was.

Then her eyes had popped open. Would he be the same

Jimmy after this? She'd find out when he called her after his return from Nashville. He would call or come over to see her, she was certain. He had sounded so sincere when he had bade her good-bye the morning after the storm.

All the next week she had waited expectantly; she had jumped every time the telephone or the doorbell had rung. Once, when she had seen the Bryant truck in the driveway she had raced downstairs, thinking the driver would be Jimmy. How silly could she have been? Of course, it wasn't. She'd never see Jimmy in that old truck again!

He didn't call and he didn't come to see her. By the end of the week she had given up hoping that he would.

He had been busy, she knew that. Upon their return from Nashville, the trio had made numerous appearances on television and radio and at local entertainments and record hops. Jimmy was certainly the most talked-about personality in town. Hardly a day passed that there wasn't an article about him and the trio in the paper.

"That boy is getting more attention in the Rocket City than the rockets are!" Papa had laughed one morning after reading another such item.

"Why not?" Dave had spoken up. "He has already reached the moon!"

Jimmy might as well be on the moon so far as she was concerned, Teddi thought unhappily.

She was cheered, however, by some good news that Mimi brought down one morning. "Mother and Daddy have decided," she said excitedly, "to come to Holston to *live!* Daddy says it's about time they settled down and put out some roots. So he is going to do what Grandmother has wanted him to do for ages—live in the big house and manage her affairs."

That Sunday Mimi had gone with the Taylors to the farm

at Redwing Crossing. Through the rose-colored glasses of happiness, she could see nothing but beauty everywhere. She had run all over the place, exclaiming joyfully at everything she saw. Dixie had introduced her to every animal on the farm, making a special effort to see that she and Cottonblossom got to know each other.

"This is really fun!" she had exclaimed as she and Dixie and Teddi picked blackberries on the bank of the creek that bordered the Taylor farm.

"I guess Cottonblossom *is* happier out here," Dixie had admitted, dropping a handful of berries into her pail while she gazed fondly at the little goat grazing on a nearby bank. "She doesn't have to be penned up and she can baa all she pleases without bothering the neighbors." Dixie had added, "Just knowing she's happy makes me feel better about giving her up."

A phone call from Jimmy would make me feel better, Teddi had thought while munching on a berry.

The news that had greeted them when they returned home had made *all* the Taylors feel better. Rock's father had decided to buy one of the Mountainside houses! And he had a friend who was being transferred with him, who was interested in another.

"I like it out there," Rock had told Teddi and Dave with real enthusiasm. "Not so ritzy as here on the Hill but I'm not really accustomed to this kind of living, anyhow."

Later Teddi had been made happier, too, when Mimi and Nancy and Viv and Carol and Ruby had accepted her invitation to come to her house for a swim. The new Mimi got along well with the girls from Colfax Street, especially Viv.

"Viv must be short for vivacious!" she had laughed while sitting in a poolside chair watching Viv dive from the board at the other end of the pool. "She is so full of pep and fun."

Teddi had glowed. She had hoped her new friends would accept her old ones, for now she knew she could never be content to have one without the other.

Grandma had always said that when moving a plant, one should always take some of the old soil with it. People and plants had a lot in common that way. When people moved, some of their past life should go with them, too. For the past enriches the present and gives it meaning.

Yes, everything had gone well, except her relationship with Jimmy.

He could call me, she had told herself mournfully a dozen times. *It only takes a second to say, "Hello, how are you?"*

Of course, she *could* call him. Or could she? It had been one thing to call the Jimmy she had known; it was quite another to call Jimmy Bryant, the recording and television star!

Now, tonight at the square dance at the Martineaux house, they would meet for the first time since they had parted after the storm. She wanted very much to see him, yet at the same time she dreaded the meeting.

Wearing the turquoise "squaw dress" with the silver rick-rack trim, she whirled before her mirror and wondered what Jimmy would think when he saw her. She had been, oh, so careful about her appearance. Her hair, brushed until it shone, had two turquoise velvet bows in it.

Jimmy had said many times that she was the prettiest girl he knew. Would he still think so, after all the girls he had met as a celebrity?

Papa whistled admiringly as she floated down the stairs. "You look just like your mother did when she was your age," he said. Teddi was pleased, for that was the highest compliment Papa could pay.

She and Rock and Nancy and Eddie and Dave and Sybil and Dixie walked together toward the big house on the Hill. Teddi was still thinking about Jimmy and their coming meeting. Would he remember, as well as she did, the last time she had worn this dress? It had been the night of the dance at the Rec Hall, when he had been so sure she would change.

Now the tables were turned. That night she had been the important one because she was moving to a fine new home. Now, he was a celebrity.

Well, she wasn't going to tell him that *he* would change—for the simple reason that he already had. Otherwise, why hadn't he called?

His certain girl. She didn't feel like that tonight.

On the steps of the portico of the Martineaux house they were met by Viv and Lyle and Carol and Bill and Jack Walker and Tess Graves. Jack introduced her to Tess. To her surprise, Tess wasn't anything like the girl she had imagined her to be. Instead of the cold, haughty creature she had expected, Teddi found a warm, charming girl.

Mimi, receiving her guests at the door, fairly sparkled. "My mother and daddy," she said proudly, introducing the handsome, graying man and lovely brown-haired woman standing beside her and her grandmother. "They came to Holston earlier than they expected so they could be here for my party!"

Then Teddi and the others went up the great staircase to the grand ballroom on the second floor. "Wow," breathed Viv as they walked in.

The others gasped. It was elaborately decorated to resemble a Western cow town at carnival time. Cardboard replicas of corrals, false-front stores, and music halls with swinging doors hung on the walls.

At one end stood a platform with a fence around it, decorated with Indian blankets, saddles, and sombreros. On the platform sat a big stereo set and Art Blake, all decked out in a dazzling white cowboy outfit.

"Still think the place looks like a museum?" Teddi teasingly asked Viv.

Viv's black eyes fairly snapped with pleasure. "Well, if it does, it's the kind I'd like to live in," she replied happily.

Teddi looked around for Jimmy—casually, as though she were taking an unusual interest in the decorations. To her disappointment Jimmy was not among the guests. Yet she felt a sense of relief at his absence, too. If he had seen her and had taken no notice of her, she would have felt awful. Now she still had hope, and hope was sweet.

The crowd kept coming. It seemed that every young person in Holston had been invited. They represented a good cross section of town, from Holly Tree Hill to Colfax Street.

At a signal from Mimi, Art Blake rose from his seat on the platform. With his usual bright chatter, he started a record turning. To the tune of "My Darling Clementine" he called a few practice maneuvers for those who hadn't square danced recently.

Teddi, and the others in her group, cheerfully went through the trial maneuvers, too. When they were over, Art told them to sit down and take a break. "We've got a real treat for you," he said.

Here it comes, Teddi thought. Sitting on a splint-bottomed rocker on the porch of the cardboard hotel, she waited anxiously.

Everyone else in the room knew what was going to happen, too, and they waited with eager expectancy. They were not disappointed. The heavy draperies at one side of the room parted. Out stepped the Jimmy Bryant trio, dressed in gay Western outfits. With broad grins they carried their instruments onto the platform, where they stood straight and then bowed. The big room boomed with applause.

Teddi, chilled and thrilled, applauded with the others. How dear and familiar Jimmy and the boys looked—and yet how strange.

When the applause died away, Jimmy stepped forward, a happy smile on his face. He bowed slightly and said, "Folks, we'd like to do our own little version of 'Comin' Round the Mountain.' And I warn you, any resemblance between it and the original is purely accidental!"

He and the boys then swung into that familiar old song and for a few bars it was recognizable. Then the lyrics changed and so did the tune. It became wild and woolly and terribly funny. Everyone was in stitches when it ended. Mrs. Martineaux and her son and daughter-in-law laughed and clapped as heartily as anyone in the room.

Jimmy waited until the audience was quiet. Then he said, "Now, we'll do 'Redwing Mountain,' and we'll do it straight."

It was followed by several other songs, done with the poise and polish of professionals.

"Those fellows have a real future ahead of them," Rock remarked, and everyone within hearing distance nodded in agreement.

Then Jimmy announced a hootenanny and asked everyone to join it. Everybody did, with happy results. Soon everyone was singing and clapping enthusiastically. Everybody except Teddi.

Jimmy hadn't indicated that he knew she was there. And she had given him plenty of chances to see her by moving to the front of her group and standing practically under his nose while he sang.

Other girls were trying to catch his attention, too. Among them were Mimi and Nancy and Tess Graves. With that kind of competition, what chance did she have? Teddi asked herself mournfully.

The boys stopped singing. "That's all for now, folks," said Jimmy. "On with the dance, Art, and I think the boys and I will do some wheeling and dealing, too. That is, if the girls are agreeable."

The squeal that went up from the girls in the room almost lifted the ceiling. Only Teddi made no sound. She was panicked.

"I doubt if you'll have any trouble getting partners," Art grinned.

Soon the strains of "Oh, Eliza, Little Liza Jane" drifted across the room and set everyone's feet tapping.

"Choose your nearest neighbor and square up!" Art called out.

Who was her nearest neighbor? Teddi thought wildly. Was it Rock? No, he was asking Mimi. Was it Jack Walker? No, he was asking Tess. They were deliberately ignoring her. Why? She turned and then she knew. Jimmy was coming toward her. Then, suddenly, he stopped and hesitated, as though in doubt whether he should ask her or not.

That he was waiting for encouragement from her was plain. Should she? He hadn't called. Still, without knowing his reasons, how could she judge him? She had jumped at so many wrong conclusions lately. Was she going to start doing so again?

No! She smiled at him, warmly and invitingly, and held out her hand. He grinned broadly and strode quickly toward her. He took her hand and squeezed it with gentle affection. Then he led her to the square being formed nearby. Rock and Mimi

smiled their welcome, and so did Viv and Lyle and Nancy
and Eddie.

> "Break into that line of four,
> Pin that line, four face four!"

Teddi and Jimmy faced each other. Suddenly it seemed as
if all the confusion and misunderstandings of the past few
weeks had been swept away.

> "Pass through."

"I thought we'd never get together again!" Jimmy's face was
earnest as it passed, close to hers.

"I thought the same thing," she replied gravely, though her
heart was singing.

> "Wheel and deal."

"I've meant to call a dozen times since I got back but it
seemed something always came up."

"That's the way I thought it must be."

His eyes were admiring. "That's the same dress you wore
the night. . . ."

"You were so sure I was going to change," she finished.

> "Box the gnat across the way."

"I was wrong."

They whirled around, changing positions. "Thank goodness,
you haven't changed," she laughed.

He raised a brow. "Why should I change?"

She shrugged. "You had as much reason as I did, with your
record and being on that Nashville show and all!"

"Oh, that! You know, I can come down as fast as I went
up! That's why, as I told you at Grandma Taylor's, I'm keeping
my feet on the ground."

A mischievous glint came into her eyes. "That's the best
place for them, don't you think?"

He squeezed her hand and laughed, "Well, that way you don't have quite so far to fall. Say, this is just like old times, isn't it?"

"Ummm." Indeed, it did seem to Teddi, as she swung from Jimmy to Eddie to Rock to Lyle and back again, just like old times at the Rec Hall. The music was the same, and the dancing, too. Around her were the same friends.

Only the glittering chandelier swinging above and the new friends she had made were different. A warm feeling stole over her. She was still Jimmy's certain girl, too!

Nothing had changed. Nothing important, anyway.